Sixgun Syndicate

SIXGUN SYNDICATE

JACKSON COLE

THORNDIKE
CHIVERS

This Large Print edition is published by Thorndike Press, Waterville, Maine, USA and by BBC Audiobooks Ltd, Bath, England.

Thorndike Press is an imprint of The Gale Group.

Thorndike is a trademark and used herein under license.

The text of this Large Print edition is unabridged.

Other aspects of the book may vary from the original edition.

Set in 16 pt. Plantin.

LIBRARY OF CONGRESS CATALOGING-IN-PUBLICATION DATA

Cole, Jackson.
 Sixgun syndicate / by Jackson Cole.
  p. cm. — (Thorndike Press large print Western)
 ISBN-13: 978-0-7862-9951-5 (hardcover : alk. paper)
 ISBN-10: 0-7862-9951-7 (hardcover : alk. paper) − 329
 1. Large type books. I. Title.
 PS3505.O2685S59 2007
 813'.52—dc22   2007034096

BRITISH LIBRARY CATALOGUING-IN-PUBLICATION DATA AVAILABLE

Published in 2007 in the U.S. by arrangement with Golden West Literary Agency.

Published in 2008 in the U.K. by arrangement with The Golden West Literary Agency.

U.K. Hardcover: 978 1 405 64356 6 (Chivers Large Print)
U.K. Softcover: 978 1 405 64357 3 (Camden Large Print)

Printed in the United States of America on permanent paper
10 9 8 7 6 5 4 3 2 1

SIXGUN SYNDICATE

CHAPTER I
DEATH WARRANTY

The posse straggled across the drainage ditch from the water-hole, the mustang hoofs kicking up droplets of wet sand, and rode toward the small, unpainted shack on the bank of the watering spot.

"Old Possum Ransom lives here," remarked a deputy named Keith Warden to another who rode beside him.

"Yeah," agreed the other deputy. "And there he is now — by the shed."

At that moment, Keith Warden felt his first qualm at having come along with Sheriff Al Craig's party. It was only instinct on the young cowboy's part, because nothing had happened, as yet.

Warden had been in Vanceville with other E P punchers who rode for "Big Ed" Pallette, owner of a great ranch, when this posse had been formed. The boss had come into the saloon and called them together, saying there was a law job to be done. Like the others, Warden had thought it would be an outlaw-chasing party, good sport while it lasted, with enough danger to spice the run. But now, it appeared, it was to be something much more distasteful.

Keith Warden lagged at the rear. Some twenty deputies followed the leaders — Sheriff Craig, Pallette, and a man named Barney Vale who was a stranger in central Texas. Among the rank and file were some punchers whom Pallette had only recently taken on, but few old-timers.

Sheriff Craig was lean and weathered. He wore a stringy, faded mustache and the deep wrinkles about his mouth were stained with tobacco juice. His battered Stetson was mouse-gray, his badge was pinned to the pocket flap of a faded shirt, and he wore old black pants and cracked boots. On his face was a serious, set look. He did not seem to like what he had to do.

Big Ed Pallette was a tall, big-boned, breezy fellow around forty. He had straight black hair, dark eyes in a long, horse face, and his complexion was dark, too. Folks called his outfit the "Epe" in pronouncing the brand.

The third man of the leaders was a quiet individual who acted more like a spectator than a member of a posse. Vale was stout, wore a dark suit, a string tie, and a narrow-brimmed felt hat. When he removed his hat to mop his brow, he exposed a bald area in his chestnut hair.

At some time his nose had been broken, so that now it was flat and broad at the bridge and, peering around this damaged appendage, were alert violet eyes. The color and calculating shrewdness of Barney Vale's eyes struck an observer instantly. And, judging by his speech, this Vale was an educated man.

Keith Warden, Pallette's young cowboy now lagging, was lean, too, but his was the leanness of vibrant strength and vitality, acquired through life in the open. His brown hair, cut short, had a healthy sheen, and his small black mustache was neatly clipped. His eyes were keen and bright, his skin bronzed by the sunlight of Texas.

He was proud of the expensive whipcord shirt and trousers, the black boots with silver spurs, and huge Stetson he wore, and of the roan gelding with the E P brand on it which he was riding. The mount was one of the string with which Pallette had provided him, as the rancher did each of his cowboys.

Warden himself might be called an educated cowboy, after a fashion, for he had had more than the average amount of schooling. He had spent a year in college, learning surveying and other subjects studied by embryo civil engineers. But the exciting life of the range had drawn him from those more sedentary activities.

"Let the hosses have a drink, Bud," Sheriff Craig ordered a cowboy riding behind him, as the posse drew rein near the water-hole. "Not too much, though. It's mighty hot, and they're lathered."

"Bud" Mason and another E P cowboy stood by to watch the mustangs, as the posse dismounted and moved toward the shack.

"Howdy, Possum!" sang out the sheriff.

He headed for the old cowman, who stared at the possemen. Pallette and Vale followed Craig over to Ransom, who shot out a long stream of tobacco juice as he waited.

"Afternoon, Al," the old man said in a rusty voice. Living alone as he did, his vocal cords were not too well-oiled.

The E P cowboys who made up the posse trailed after their leaders, but stopped a dozen feet away. They had no orders, so waited silently, some of them — like Keith Warden — uncomfortably. They were aware that "Possum" Ransom was an old nuisance, that he interfered with the sweep of the great E P, as did other comparatively small landholders in the vicinity. But most of them wished him no harm.

"Possum," said Craig, in a worried voice. "I told yuh to get a lawyer and see to yore title here." The sheriff was a plodding honest man. He was not too bright, but he was a stickler for upholding the law.

"Shucks!" snapped Ransom. "I was here before Pallette. Been here fifty-one years come next July."

Possum Ransom was eccentric. No one doubted that. But he was not crazy, and he had lived here long before Keith Warden, for one, was born. Possum had been the first settler in the section.

"Yuh didn't take my advice," growled Craig. "Now I got a dispossess to hand yuh, Possum. I hate to do it. We been good friends. But the law's the law."

"Yuh mean I got to shift to please Pallette?"

Ransom scowled at the horse-faced E P boss, who scowled back. There was bad blood between the two — arguments over fenced water, missing calves and so on.

"Yuh can't show a warranty deed or paper, can yuh, Possum, to prove this is yore land?" demanded Craig. "Pallette owns it — now."

Possum Ransom dropped a gnarled hand to the holstered Frontier Model Colt revolver. It was one of the early models, an antique, thought Warden.

"This here is my title!" old Possum said hotly. "Yuh can't do no such a thing to me! Go on — get, Pallette!"

Snarling, Ransom pulled the gun — a mistake, no doubt. There was a sudden movement, a pistol blared. Possum Ransom went down, a dazed look in his bleared eyes. The Frontier Model fell in the sand, and Possum's neck was limp.

It was Barney Vale who had shot Ransom dead. Vale held a short-barreled, large-caliber pistol of newest make in his hand.

"I had to shoot, Sheriff," he said shortly. "He was going to fire at us. It was self-defense."

The cowboys stared, shocked. They saw the poor bundle of what had been a harmless old fellow lying by his unpainted shack. Warden was horrified.

Craig swore, jumped forward, bent over Possum Ransom.

"He's dyin'!" he cried. "Yuh hit him in the heart, I reckon, Vale. Yuh shouldn't have done it."

"The old fool would have hurt somebody," insisted Barney Vale. "It was self-defense."

"I don't believe he'd of shot," said Craig, shaking his head sadly. "It was a bluff."

But the fact remained that Ransom had first drawn his pistol and, technically, Vale was correct.

Big Ed Pallette found his voice.

"He's a goner," he rumbled, "and I'll swear that Vale saved us from the old hombre's slugs!"

He turned to frown at his cowboys. They understood. That was the Boss's stand.

Some of the new E P men were grinning. For some reason Ransom's death amused them. They were tough, these recent additions to the E P, and did not mingle with Pallette's established crew. Big Ed had let some of his veterans go to make room for these men, and since they had been taken on Barney Vale had taken to hanging around a lot with Pallette.

Vale seemed to have a hold over the owner of the E P, and over the new punchers also.

After a while the posse rod away. Possum Ransom had died quickly, and Craig left two deputies to bury the old fellow.

Keith Warden didn't like what had happened at all. Possum Ransom had irritated him at times, but he could not condone the old man's killing.

He tagged along, with his particular knot

of friends, at the rear again. They had hard looks for Barney Vale's back, but the tough gang which Pallette had been hiring did not seem depressed by the shooting. They hung together behind Barney Vale.

Sheriff Craig's party rode westward and came out on a rough dirt road, which they followed, with the sheriff, Vale and Pallette still in front. Turning up a lane, they approached a square, white-painted ranchhouse, a small place but a well-kept one. It had a barn, sheds, and corrals.

"Lew Garrett's," growled young Warden's cowboy comrade. "Wonder why they're stoppin' here?"

"Don't know," said Warden. "But I do know Big Ed don't cotton to Garrett, either. I savvy the boss'd like to grab this stretch. It slices up his range, even more'n what Ransom's does."

Possum Ransom's home lay west of Pallette's spread, and Garrett's place was west of the old squatter's.

Lew Garrett was a strong, big-bodied man of middle-age. He looked anxious as he came out, seeing the posse pull up in his front yard.

"I don't like this at all," muttered Warden.

He meant to keep an eye on Vale this time. If Vale went for his gun, Warden was determined to prevent the man who was a stranger, here anyhow, from killing anybody.

The sheriff got down heavily, followed by Big Ed Pallette and Barney Vale. They faced Lew Garrett.

"Afternoon, Garrett," greeted the sheriff. "Yuh savvy why we're here, I reckon. Yuh had notice before that yore title was no good. Are yuh ready to move?" This was as distasteful to Craig as the scene at Ransom's had been, but such proceedings were part of a sheriff's duty.

Keith Warden listened, watched, and he grew more interested as he saw a girl emerge from the open front door of the house to join Garrett.

Sue Garrett was the rancher's daughter, and a mighty pretty one, Warden thought — a strawberry blonde with wide-set, amber eyes. The sun caught her thick, piled hair as she came from the porch. She wore a plain blue dress which set off her girlish figure, and the garment's simplicity accentuated the girl's attractiveness. She had some freckles across her nose, and on her pink cheeks, and they showed vividly now, because she was angry as she hurried to her father and glared at the men confronting him. As though to back him, she took hold of her father's arm.

15

A slim, red-haired, keen-eyed young fellow in cowboy rig came out on the veranda and leaned against a post. Keith Warden knew him — Frank Garrett, who was two or three years younger than his sister Sue.

"There's some mistake, Craig," Lew Garrett was protesting vehemently. "I filed my claim at Austin in the regular way, twenty years ago! This is my property. Yuh've got no right to try to shoo us off."

"He's worried sick," thought Warden, for he could read the misery in Garrett's eyes. Because for all the man's defiant talk it was plain that he was not sure of his stand.

"We've heard all that, Garrett," growled Pallette. "Yuh've told us before. But there ain't no record in Austin that yuh ever proved yore homestead. Mebbe yuh forgot. Anyway, that ain't my hard luck. I've bought the property from the legal owner, who had the genuine warranty and all, set down properlike at the General Land Office in Austin."

Garrett drew in a deep breath of the warm air, air which was his — or which he had long believed to be his. A man grew to love his home, his soil, the familiar buildings and the trees. He was obviously trying to control himself, but his face was red, his fists clenched.

16

"We recorded in Austin, I tell yuh!" he insisted. "Yuh'll have to give me more time. Somethin's gone wrong!"

"Time!" cried Pallette. "Yuh had plenty notice."

"I'm a land expert, Garrett," Barney Vale spoke up coldly. "My office is in Austin. I've gone into this thoroughly. You are now on Pallette's land, with no legal right to be here."

Pallette and Vale irritated Garrett. His rage was for Big Ed and the land agent, rather than for Craig, who was only carrying out his duties.

"Somehow or other," growled Garrett, "the papers got mixed up at Austin. That'll have to be straightened out. I ain't goin' to move. Pallette, you want my ranch to round out yore spread. Yuh're a hog, and yuh ain't goin' to get away with it!"

"Keep a civil tongue in yore head or yuh'll get it blowed off!" snapped Pallette.

Warden tensed, ready for trouble.

"Now, now, gents," Sheriff Craig said quickly. "Take it easy!"

"I ought to punch yore face in!" cried Garrett, taking a step toward Pallette. He had the Texan's individualistic instinct to fight for his rights.

Sue tugged at her father's arm, holding

him back.

"Dad, stop it! This won't get you any-where!" She had a nice voice, but she was an angry girl.

She looked with flaming eyes at Pallette and Barney Vale.

"You're thieves, both of you!" she accused hotly. "You've stolen our home from us! I don't know how you worked it, but it's true."

The voices raised in anger had brought Mrs. Garrett from the house. She came down the steps, past her son Frank who had not moved since he had paused on the porch. But a Colt pistol was in his holster and he plainly was ready for a fight.

Mrs. Garrett's hair was graying now, though it had been like her daughter's. She wore a calico dress, with an apron tied about the waist of her ample figure.

"Lew, there's no use!" she called. "You come back in here."

Garrett wanted to fight, but his daughter and wife held him back. He was used to listening to them.

"All right," he grunted.

"Yuh got to shift, Garrett," repeated Craig firmly, but he was relieved that the threat of battle had been temporarily checked.

"We'll move by next Monday," promised

18

Garrett dully.

"Don't try to take any of the buildings or damage 'em in any way," said Barney Vale. "They belong to the owner of the land."

Instantly Garrett was choking with rage again, but Sue kept a tight hold on his arm. Her mother was at the rancher's other side.

"That'll do," Craig said shortly, and nodded. "All right, boys. We'll ride. We'll be back to take possession Monday, Garrett."

"Wait a minute, Sheriff," interrupted Vale. "Yuh've got the legal dispossess on yuh. Why not serve it now and save collecting another posse next week?"

But Craig could be pushed just so far.

"I've given him till next Monday, Vale," he said sullenly.

The sheriff turned to his horse, mounted, and signaled to his men to ride.

CHAPTER II
TROUBLE IS NEAR

Keith Warden felt guilty. He was ashamed to be in the company of such men as Vale and Pallette. His boss had not shown up well today.

The puncher glanced back, biting his crisp mustache. He could see the Garretts, with Lew's wife and daughter on either side of him.

"Ed Pallette, you're a thief!" red-headed Sue Garrett called after them.

Young Warden was glum all the way on the ride back to Vanceville. Once there, when the posse split up and wandered toward the saloons, the waddy himself headed straight for his boss, Big Ed Pallette.

"I want my time, Ed," he said coldly.

Pallette frowned at him.

"Yeah? What's wrong? Don't yuh like the grub at the Epe?"

Warden stared straight into Big Ed's deep-set eyes. The boss was angry, but after a silent moment he looked away, backed down. He had worn a brash front, but Warden wondered if inwardly Pallette was not ashamed of himself.

"All right, Warden," Big Ed muttered. "I'll pay yuh off."

The rancher realized the futility of arguing. This disgusted cowboy was quitting. He would ride to the E P, get his own horse and belongings, and leave.

Which Warden lost no time in doing. Waiting only long enough to give the roan gelding a breather, he mounted and headed out of town. . . .

The night was several hours old when Lewis Garrett, the small rancher who had been dispossessed by Pallette and Vale, entered Vanceville. He rode through a back street, careful to keep in the shadows. Most of the houses were quiet and dark, but there were lights on in several saloons. From the largest of the lot, the Golden Horns, music sounded. Inside the place cowboys and townsmen were drinking, playing cards, or tripping the more or less light fantastic with the girls who worked for the Golden Horns.

Garrett dropped the reins of his big horse up the way from the back door of the saloon. On foot, he moved toward the place. He was angry all through now, angry at what had been done to him under the cover of the law, but he was keeping a grip on his temper. He meant to do his best to fight back at those who had robbed him and his family.

It took a little time for him to locate Big Ed Pallette and the stranger named Barney Vale. At last he found them drinking and talking together, in a private room at the rear of the Golden Horns.

Through a window Garrett saw Pallette slumped in his chair. The rancher had been imbibing heavily all evening, and his voice was thick. Garrett first caught the man's words in the middle of a sentence.

"— tell you, I'm mighty worried, Vale. Yuh reckon it's all safe and legal-like, what we're doin'? Yuh shore there won't be no trouble?"

Vale was impatient.

"I've told you a hundred times you don't need to worry, Pallette. I've taken care of everything."

"But s'posin' Garrett and others find out yuh done took them papers."

Garrett, close to the open window now, listened with bated breath. He had been sure Vale and Pallette had conspired in some dishonest way, and here was the proof. His heart picked up its beat. Then it gave a terrible leap, as he felt a gun muzzle rammed

22

into his spine, heard a harsh voice saying:

"Reach, you!"

Garrett put up his hands. The talk inside the room stopped, and Barney Vale hurried to the window.

"What is it, Mike?" demanded Vale, sticking out his head and shoulders.

"I caught this hombre snoopin', Barney," said the man called Mike.

"Oh — it's you, Garrett!" drawled Vale.

"You thief!" snapped Garrett.

Vale went out the window, agilely. He moved in a quick, sure way.

Suddenly Garrett realized just how dangerous Vale was.

"No, yuh don't!" gasped the small rancher.

Vale had whipped out a pistol, the same one with which he had killed Possum Ransom, and instantly it was shoved into Garrett's body. It blared, muffled by the closeness to Garrett's clothing and flesh. Lew Garrett slumped against the wall. His mouth was open but no sounds came forth.

Music from the dance hall, and the raucous sounds made by the merrymakers had almost drowned out the revolver's muffled explosion.

Mike bent over Garrett. "Good glory, Barney!" he muttered. "Yuh've killed him!"

■ ■ ■ ■

"Land, land, land! It's a great invention —
but it shore causes a heap of trouble!"

Captain Bill McDowell spoke aloud,
though no one was listening as he stared at
the map of Texas on his office wall in Austin. As chief of the Texas Rangers, McDowell had proved his ability in his younger days
when he had convinced sundry outlaws and
Indian raiders that the climate of the Lone
Star State was unhealthy for such.

Now, too old and crippled to leap on a
mustang and gallop to the scene of a crime,
there to mete out justice on the spot, Mc-
Dowell planned strategy in foiling outlaws
who sought to infest the country. But he
had to order others to carry out his ideas.
These ideas were germinated by the com-
plaints which flowed to headquarters, com-
plaints from injured people, Texans.

The map on the wall, though only a few
feet square, represented a lot of land. Texas
was eight hundred miles across, and as
broad as the distance between the Red River
and the Rio Grande. The land was not flat,
like the map. It was hilly here, flat there,
wet and black on the Gulf coast and northeast, red in the north, gray and other hues

in the south, rocky, with stretches of desert-like sections across the Pecos which were as large as many Eastern states.

There were mountains ten thousand feet high, and swamps and lagoons below sea level. Some of the land was so akin to the popular conception of Hades, that no one could pay men to try and dwell on it. On the other hand, great, rolling districts were fertile. Cotton, wheat and other valuable crops would spring up, while the grassy ranges would support untold cattle herds.

Yet all this, as well as the mineral wealth which had already been discovered and that as yet was unguessed at beneath the land, had been without the slightest value *per se* until men had come to settle on it, to raise families, to wrangle and fight. There had to be some order to it, this land-thirst which mankind evinced; it had to be controlled. So titles had been invented, a land office set up in Austin, making it necessary for anyone claiming desired acreage to register his grant.

Complicating it all, in Texas, was the fact that the land in question had successively belonged to Spain, Mexico, the Republic of Texas, the Confederacy, and the United States. And many Texans possessed the breezy characters which made them cocksure, certain they could protect themselves and their property without benefit of law.

"If I had an army about the size of General Lee's," mused McDowell, "mebbe in time I could tame, curry and hang the State out to dry."

Instead of an army, though, he had a handful of Texas Rangers — great officers, every man, but they had vast distances to cover. Far away, a journey which took weeks, lay El Paso, and the Apaches raided from old Mexico when the moon was up. Outlaws made flying runs from Indian Territory and Oklahoma, and there were plenty of local lights who belonged behind the strongest steel bars yet invented.

McDowell picked up the letter he had just received, and read it again. It had been written in a fine feminine hand, but there was rather a shaky look to some of the letters, and at the bottom corner was a discolored spot. That spot, the old Ranger Captain was sure, had been made by a woman's tear, falling as she wept for her dead husband.

It started a spark within McDowell which, igniting, became a slow fire, which swiftly leaped into a blaze, until within him was a raging conflagration of anger.

He leaped to his feet with a curse, began pacing his office, back and forth, ten paces over, ten back, a pause to stamp his booted foot. The cool blue eyes sparked now. When he became overheated, it was always like this. Captain Bill McDowell exploded.

"Cuss it!" he raved, "I can't figger it out from here! Hatfield's here. I'll have to send him, even if he did just get in from a tough trip. It ain't so far off as usual, this trouble."

McDowell stopped muttering to himself, and raised his chin.

"You outside there!" he howled. "Send Ranger Hatfield in, pronto!"

The clerk jumped from his stool with a guilty start. He had been looking out the window for a moment. McDowell's voice told him the Captain was bellowing mad, and he hastened to inform the Ranger.

Soon Jim Hatfield, McDowell's star officer, walked into headquarters and to McDowell's office. He moved with a pantherish, quiet tread as he entered the room.

Hatfield towered as he stood there in the middle of the floor. For he was well over six feet, with wide shoulders, though they tapered to the fighting man's narrow waist.

Hatfield wore a clean blue shirt and fresh bandanna, and whipcord trousers tucked into spurred, polished boots. The chin-strap runner of his big Stetson was loose under his rugged jaw. He had jet-black hair sheening with the oil of youth, and somber, gray-green eyes.

Power was written all over him, but the severity of his face was relieved by a wide mouth, which indicated innate good humor. He carried well-tended Colt .45s in the supple holsters which were attached to the cartridge belts. Bronzed as an Inca image by the wind and sun of Texas, Hatfield was Texas manhood at its peak.

The almost lazy way he carried himself in repose belied his real swiftness in action. For those slender hands of his could whip out and shoot the Colts in his holsters with blinding speed.

McDowell always felt comforted when Hatfield was near. He knew he could count on the Ranger as he once could on himself to carry out a mission.

"How are yuh?" he growled. "Sort of rested?"

"Yes, suh." Hatfield had a soft, drawling voice, almost gentle. "Couldn't feel better, Cap'n Bill."

"Bueno." McDowell passed over the letter. "Read this from a Mrs. Garrett. They had a ranch near Vanceville and it was took away from 'em. Her husband was shot and killed, but she ain't shore who done it. She suspects a big rancher named Pallette might savvy.

Seems this Pallette, who owns a spread he calls the E P over there, has been cleanin' out smaller fry who was in his way when he wanted to expand. This Mrs. Garrett claims her husband did file their land, but somethin's gone wrong about the deed. And there was another shootin', she says. An old feller named Possum Ransom, a squatter. Vanceville ain't far, Jim — not a hundred miles — so yuh could make it in twenty-four hours."

Hatfield looked at the letter again, carefully noting the names and places mentioned.

"I'll run over for a look-see right off, Cap'n," he said. "Sounds like high-handed business."

"Go to it. Let me hear what's up. It's got queer angles to it I ain't run into before."

The Ranger nodded. When Captain Bill hadn't heard of something, it must be unique indeed, for the old captain's experience ran the gamut of human experiences.

With all the facts available in Austin at his command, Jim Hatfield shook hands with McDowell and strolled outside. In the sunshine Hatfield inhaled a deep breath of the warm, aromatic air. He loved the outdoors, the wild danger trails he rode. They were life to him.

In the shade stood his golden sorrel, the companion of many adventures. Goldy was a magnificent, long-legged, untiring animal, as intelligent in his own way as the Ranger was in his.

He was saddled, waiting for Hatfield, and greeted him by nosing the Ranger's hand and sniffing. A carbine rode in a sling under one of Hatfield's long legs as he mounted. There were iron rations in his saddle-bags, a fresh shirt or two, and a poncho was rolled at the cantle.

Equipped for any campaign, Hatfield waved a hand to old McDowell, who stared nostalgically from the window, wishing that he, too, were riding.

CHAPTER III
INTERRUPTED LYNCH PARTY

Ranger Hatfield rode along the dirt lane toward a square, white-painted ranchhouse, a small place, but one which looked as though it had been cared for lovingly. But the wooden signpost, which said "Lewis Garrett," at the entrance to the private way, was filled with fresh bullet-holes, as though men had been using it for a target.

In a corral at one side mustangs moved about, and on the front veranda saddles and other gear, as well as a stack of heavy rifles had been piled. A couple of heavy-jowled, thick-set men in leather clothing and big hats sat there. They stared fixedly at the tall officer on the golden sorrel as he approached.

Only the day before yesterday, Hatfield had been called by Captain McDowell and despatched from Austin. The Ranger had made the run easily. He had found time to sleep and rest the sorrel, and now was spruced up, shaved and clean. He had made inquiries about how to find the Garrett place, for he had decided to call on Mrs. Lewis Garrett first of all, even before talking to Sheriff Craig in Vanceville. After all, she was the chief complainant.

Now he was here, but he saw no sign of Mrs. Garrett.

He could hear a raucous, drunken voice which apparently meant to be jovial, howling inside the house:

"Yo-ho-ho and a keg of red-eye!"

The Garrett ranch did not have the air of decency the Ranger had expected. He was suspicious, ready for trouble, as one of the burly men on the porch sang out:

"Hey there, stranger! Lookin' for somebody?"

The two toughs were watching him from across the low railing around the veranda. Colts showed in their oiled holsters. Their hands were calloused, dirty, their eyes hard. There were other men in the house. Hatfield could glimpse them through the open windows.

"Garretts ain't here, are they?" Hatfield drawled.

"Garretts?" repeated the man who had hailed him. The fellow's jutting jaw needed a shave. He wore twin, blue-steel pistols with smooth walnut stocks. "Never heard of 'em."

The other man on the veranda considered this humorous. His lips twitched back and Hatfield glimpsed tobacco-stained teeth.

The Ranger kept his temper. "The sign says this is the place I want, and I was directed here. I'm huntin' a job punchin' cows and was told mebbe they'd take me on."

"Garretts done moved," volunteered the man with the stained teeth.

"Yuh savvy where they went to?" asked Hatfield.

"Yuh're shore a questionin' son, ain't yuh?" remarked the fellow with the jutting jaw, determined to have his joke at any cost. "What yuh think we are — an information bu-row? How in blazes can we keep track of such folks?"

Hatfield eyed him coolly. He saw that men had come to the open windows, and to the doorway, for a look at whoever was outside. They were of the same stamp as the two on the porch, though of different shapes and sizes. Some were bearded, others simply dirty of face. All were heavily armed, steel-eyed, the sort of men who would be ready for a fight any time. The vocalist was still rendering his song, tearing it apart now.

33

"We don't know where the Garretts went to," Stained Teeth said hastily. "But if yuh're huntin' a ridin' job, why not try Pallette's Epe? Yuh must of seen his brand sign when yuh passed there, if yuh come on the east-west road."

"That's right, I did. Yuh reckon he'd take me on?"

"If yuh'd quit partin' yore hair in the middle," observed the humorist, "and quit singin' sopranner, yuh might do."

This was too much for Heavy Jowl's partner, who bust into a guffaw.

"Yuh're shore a card, Henny! Singin' so-pranner!" He smote his leather-clad thigh in a frenzy of amusement.

"Yuh're a ring-ting-tootin' little joker, ain't yuh?" drawled the Ranger. "I ain't felt so tickled since my last uncle dropped dead."

There was no sense in maintaining a polite front with such men. They looked on ordinary courtesy as cowardice.

The wind taken out of his sails, the jester grew stern and mean.

"Go on — get Sonny," he snarled. "This is private property. Hightail! We don't cotton to strangers."

All the men were ready, arms hanging limp at their sides, watching every move

Hatfield made. There was no use in starting a gun battle under such conditions. They could pick him off from the windows without any trouble, and he had no cause, as yet, to battle them.

He gave a short nod, a shrug, turned the sorrel, and started away. His back to them might be an invitation, but he had to chance it.

He was twenty-five yards from the porch when he heard the close shriek of a six-shooter bullet, then the crisp crack of the revolver. He whirled in his saddle. Mr. Joker had sent that hurrying slug after him.

" 'scuse me, suh," called the jester. "My foot slipped!"

Laughter came from his audience, and the tough was vastly pleased with himself. Hatfield rode calmly on. The Garrett place was in enemy hands — that was plain.

A quarter-mile from the little ranch, a horseman approached the Ranger. Hatfield saw his dust and was on the alert. A rider on a rangy brown horse galloped up. He wore leather, a strapped Stetson, pistols, and a short-barreled rifle was under one leg.

All in all, he looked as though he might be of the same breed as the men at Garrett's. When he came close to the tall officer, he was watchful, did not take his dark-lined eyes off the Ranger. But as Hatfield made no attempt to stop him, he flashed by, with a quick wave of the hand, and sped on along the road.

"Seems in a powerful hurry," mused Hatfield.

Dust hung in the air over the highway. Hatfield's gray-green eyes sought the hill a few hundred yards from the margin of the road. It was a covert of long-needled, short pines, and would make a good observation point.

"I'll see what holds, I reckon," he remarked to Goldy.

From the hill he could see the Garrett ranch. Sure enough, the rider turned in there, and rode on to the house.

Hatfield had not long to wait, before a dozen horsemen, having saddled up at the corral, came back along the road, passing the point where the Ranger had swung off. Among them were the two with whom he had spoken at the ranch.

"That first hombre was a messenger or scout," decided the Ranger. "He's called his pards out and, judgin' from their looks, it ain't for a tea-party."

Letting them have a start, Hatfield returned to the road and leisurely trailed after them.

They left the highway after a short run, and cut northward over broken country, grassy areas, sliced by wooded draws and rocky sections. He kept after them, taking care to stay out of their sight. He could move by riding behind natural contours.

The bunch, led by the messenger, knew just where to go. Out on a flat stretch stood a cowpony, reins to the ground. Some hundred yards away was a slim young man in tan whipcord trousers, a heavy shirt, a big Stetson, and boots whose polished sides sheened in the sunlight. He looked like a cowboy, but was busy squinting along the sights of a transit, a surveyor's instrument. He had with him stakes, poles, and other equipment needed to determine land boundaries.

So absorbed was the young man in his task that the dozen toughs from the former Garrett ranch were almost upon him before he knew they were coming. For on the west edge of the flat was an outcropping, rocks and clay, overgrown with brush, and the gunslingers had come up behind it, and cut through a narrow gap.

The surveyor suddenly caught the thud of hoofs, glanced up and saw them. Their carbines and rifles were trained on him. His horse stood too far away for him to hope to reach the mount. He froze where he was.

Hatfield, using the same cover the attackers had, approached as rapidly as possible. He dismounted at the gap, seized his carbine, and took up a position in the rocks, on the side nearer to the flat stretch. The wind was his way, and he could hear their loud voices.

"What yuh doin' here, cuss yuh?" shouted the leader of the bunch — the joker.

"I'm practisin' surveyin'," the cowboy told him. "Done studied it some and I didn't want to get rusty."

A laugh greeted this. They evidently knew he was lying.

Hatfield, his carbine cradled in his left arm as he squatted in the bush, thought the young fellow held himself well. He didn't show the fear which must have seized him as he found himself caught.

"He looks like a rustler to me," observed another gunhand.

"That's right!" yelped another. "I know him now. He's Blackjack Warden, the Terror of Tuscaloosa! I savvy him. Let's give him what he deserves!"

It was crude, cruel humor. A couple of riders had jumped from their saddles, to come up behind the cowboy and snatch his pistol. Another, with the rustler angle introduced, quickly readied a lariat, and dropped the loop over the young man's head.

The would-be humorist, the burly tough with whom Hatfield had exchanged words, picked up the transit, and smashed it over the victim's head and shoulders. The instrument was broken, and the cowboy's Stetson caved in. The force of the blow knocked the victim off his feet.

The two men holding the rope hauled on it. They ran toward the rocks where Hatfield was hidden, followed by the bunch. Most of them were grinning, having a good time at this deadly sport.

A pine, with a limb high enough for their purpose, was growing at the base of the rocks, and one of the ropers began tossing the lariat end. He missed the branch a couple of times, then the long rope went over, was seized and jerked tight. The unfortunate cowboy was lifted clear of the ground, his neck nearly broken. He got his hands up, clawing frantically at the tight noose to keep from strangling.

"Let him down for a jiffy," growled the vicious leader. "We'll have to tie the cuss's hands."

"Let's use him for a target while he's kickin'!" suggested another.

"Drop it and reach, gents!" commanded the Ranger.

The voice, slow and drawling in normal conversation, had an incisive, commanding note which struck straight home with the chilling stab of a stiletto point. Each outlaw in the bunch believed he had been directly threatened, and froze in his tracks. The cowboy sprawled on the earth, gasping for wind, clawing at the rope around his throat.

"I can take most of yuh with me if yuh rush me," Hatfield threatened.

He was close, but they could see only the black muzzle of the steady carbine trained on them.

"Who are you, and what yuh want?" demanded the joker, after a moment.

"I want you boys to clear out," Hatfield said, in a cold, deadly voice. "Leave that feller lie. If yuh try to hurt him any more, I'll kill ev'ry cuss in yore outfit! Savvy?"

CHAPTER IV
IMPORTANT
INFORMATION

The outlaws considered their unexpected predicament for a few breaths of time. If the man in the rocks was alone, they could get him in a concerted rush, but if he was anything of a marksman, it would mean several dead and wounded. They decided that the game was not worth the risk. They could try another time.

"All right," said the man who had been called Henny, his eyes narrowed. He turned slowly away, but kept his hands up. Back over his shoulder, he called, "Can we have our hosses?"

"Yeah. Go to 'em, mount and ride off. Keep a-goin'."

The men of the tough bunch were angry, and shamefaced at their defeat, but they trailed across the flat, and took to saddles. Now and then one would glance at the rocks in which the Ranger crouched.

"Yuh'll pay for this, whoever yuh are!"

howled the joker, shaking his fist from the back of his horse. Hatfield sent a carbine slug over his head, so close it nearly ventilated the peak of the fellow's Stetson.

"Excuse me," he called. "My foot slipped."

Some of them were already spurring off. But the leader heard that, and knew who it was in the rocks. The gang rode away.

"Hey you, down there!" called the Ranger to the cowboy. "Can yuh reach yore hoss?"

"Yeah, I'm not hurt much."

The waddy's voice was hoarse with rage, his face as red as flame. He had the loop from around his throat, but on his neck were several scarlet burns which had been made by the rope. His hand went to his empty holster. His overpowering impulse was to fight, to send lead after the men who had come so close to killing him.

He got up on one knee, pushed to his feet with his hand. He was dizzy, and kept shaking his head. He was a good-looking young man, with crisp brown hair and a clipped mustache. He also had fine features, and carried himself with a resolute air.

Hatfield watched him carefully. As the cowboy, in his spurred boots, started to run awkwardly for his gray gelding, some of the enemy opened fire at long range. Spurts of dirt leaped up around the running man.

Hatfield threw up his carbine and answered. His bullets were accurate, and he was shooting from a steady stance. A mustang gave a great leap, began fighting the bit. A tough snatched at his shoulder, bent to one side with pain as a hunk of lead slashed his flesh. The outlaw bunch quit trying to kill the cowboy, and spurred off.

Now the man the Ranger had snatched from death was in the saddle, reins up. He rode with practised grace, and the gray horse was a fine animal. He came galloping to the rocks, and Hatfield signaled him through the gap.

For the first time, as the Ranger rose and went to the path, the two came face to face. The cowboy stared with deep curiosity at the tall officer.

"So you're the man who saved my bacon!" he explained. "I'm shore grateful, mister."

"Forget it." Such thanks embarrassed the Ranger. "What's yore handle?"

"Warden, Keith Warden. I was surveyin' out there when them lobos come up on me, and I —"

"Let's ride first, and talk as we go," suggested Hatfield. "They're beginnin' to circle now and they'll mebbe try for us again."

Warden nodded. He kept licking his lips, clearing his throat for that rope had been mighty uncomfortable. Now and then the waddy gave an involuntary shudder.

Hatfield whistled, and the golden sorrel trotted to him. He mounted and, with Warden at his side, they moved swiftly off.

"Here they come!" Warden said swiftly. "They're tryin' to cut us off from the road!"

"I ain't too familiar with these parts," said the Ranger. "What's the best way for us to run?"

"I'd say west, but let's keep in the open. We don't want to come too close to Garrett's — I mean, the ranch them killers have took over."

Goldy and Warden's gray were superior runners. They could outdistance anything of the usual mustang variety so, taking the turn as Warden suggested, the two young men picked up speed. The killers kept doggedly after them for a time, but the range was too long for any kind of shooting.

"My handle is Hays — Jim Hays — Warden," Hatfield said after a while, in answer to the cowboy's natural query. "I was passin' through and saw 'em workin' on yuh."

It was the Ranger's way not to reveal his name at once, when he first entered new territory, but to study a case carefully before announcing his calling. In this way, Hatfield could uncover the truth, and the enemy would have no warning that a Texas Ranger was on the spot.

Warden was quite willing to talk. And why not? The tall man on the sorrel had after all, just given him back the life of which he had despaired.

"They're gunhands, yeah," explained Warden. "They're on Big Ed Pallett's payroll but they ain't regular waddies at all. They're hired for strong-arm work and killin'. That Garrett ranch belonged to some good friends of mine. It stood in Pallette's way, like others, and by some sort of crooked work, the Garretts were run off. Lew Garrett hisself was killed one night in Vanceville. I don't doubt Pallette or Vale done it — mebbe both of 'em."

"Vale?" repeated the Ranger. "He another big rancher?"

"No, Barney Vale don't belong hereabouts. But ever since he showed up he's been workin' hand in glove with Big Ed Pallette. Vale's some sort of land shark, I believe. I saw him shoot down Possum Ransom, an old squatter who had a shack up the line. Vale claimed Possum meant to kill the sheriff and Pallette, but — Well, he was a funny old cuss, Possum, cantankerous mebbe, but no harm to anybody."

"What makes you think Vale and Pallette

might have downed Garrett?" Hatfield asked, curiously.

"I don't know. It's my hunch — got no proof. Yuh see, Garrett was mighty sore, the way things went. He had a clean title, from all I can find out, but it couldn't be found registered in Austin, though Garrett swore he'd done all the law said he must do to cinch his hold on the land. He went to town, and I believe it was to try and check upon Vale and Pallette. Then he was found, shot dead, and dumped in a gutter. It was an awful blow to his wife and kids."

"Where's this Mrs. Garrett and the rest of the family now?" asked Hatfield.

"Livin' with a cousin about fifteen miles west of here. I been stayin' there myself, when I ain't workin'. Today I was checkin' boundaries, surveyin', so's to see what's what."

"Yuh savvy civil engineerin'? I know a bit myself."

"I studied a while, before I turned cowhand," explained Warden. "I can handle a transit and lay out corners and so on."

Hatfield glanced back over his big, hunched shoulder. The gun bunch were still plugging along on their trail, but they were losing distance and did not look as dangerous as they had when closer.

The Ranger congratulated himself on having snatched Keith Warden from death. Not only had he saved a splendid young Texan, but he had gained a valuable ally who was supplying him with the vital information he needed. He found Warden's character a pleasing one, for he believed the cowboy to be courageous, shrewd, genuine.

Warden indicated some bunches of cattle off to the right.

"E P stock," he informed Hatfield. "They call the spread the Epe. I rode for Pallette till he got ambitious and started wipin' out small folks in his way. Lot of the boys quit, when I did. They got strong stomachs, but it was too much. Now Pallette hires toughs, like yuh seen stringin' me up. They'd have killed me in a few minutes."

They kept going. After a few more miles of the hopeless chase, the joker and his merrymen shook their fists at the two, and cut south. Warden grinned triumphantly.

"They've quit!" he said exultantly. "They're on their way back to Garrett's old ranch. What say we head for Tate's? Mrs. Tate is that cousin of Mrs. Garrett's. That's where Sue Garrett and her mother are stayin'. We can rest up there and eat."

"*Bueno.*" Hatfield wished to see Mrs. Garrett, widow of the rancher, who had been mysteriously killed. "Yuh got any idea what the handle of that chunky hombre is — the one who was so anxious to see you kick air?"

"That sidewinder? They call him Five-Finger Henny, on account he always measures his drinks to five fingers. He's a tough one."

The Ranger was considering the situation with deep seriousness. Those killers had caught Warden, who was already in trouble because he had told off Pallette, snooping on the range. Probably they had been given orders to kill the cowboy, who had thrown in his lot with the Garretts.

The afternoon was well along when the two young fellows rode into the yard at Tate's little ranch. At once the Ranger realized what powerful lure had drawn Keith Warden to toss in his lot with the Garretts — as soon as his eyes lit on Sue Garrett.

Sue had been watching for Warden. It was easy to tell that by the way she jumped from her chair, by the smile which lighted her face. Hatfield had an eye for a pretty girl, and knew this one was exceptional. She came toward them now, as they dismounted, crossing the yard. She was animated, and Hatfield caught just one glimpse of her amber eyes, before they went past his face to Warden's.

"I was getting worried, Keith," Sue said quickly. "Did you have any trouble?"

"A little," Warden confessed. "But Jim Hays here got me out of it, Sue. This is Sue Garrett, Jim."

The girl acknowledged the introduction politely, but she was anxious to know what had happened to Warden.

"I knew it!" she cried, when he told her what had occurred. "You mustn't risk your life by going over there any more, do you hear?"

Warden grinned, winking at the Ranger.

They took care of the horses, then followed Sue into the house. The Tate place was a small outfit, but it controlled a small lake and part of the brook running from it. George Tate was an elderly, steady-looking Texan. He had three sons and several daughters, and with the help of two hired hands, they ran the ranch.

In the small but comfortable home, Hatfield was introduced by Warden to Mrs. Garrett. The Ranger smiled down at the widow of the wronged rancher. She did not know — yet — that it was her complaint which had brought Hatfield here from Austin.

She was around fifty, and had a comfortable, ample figure. Her hair was graying, but she was still an attractive woman. The Ranger could see where Sue got her good looks. The mother showed the terrible shock and strain she had undergone. It was plain in her eyes, her manner.

It had not been long since her husband had died violently in Vanceville. Yet she had gained control of herself. She greeted Hatfield heartily, as Warden began to tell them all about the events of the afternoon.

The room was crowded with Tates — boys and girls, young men and women. Mrs. Tate came from the kitchen, where she was preparing the evening meal. When it was learned that the tall stranger with Warden had saved the cowboy's life, nothing was too good for him. Drink was brought, pressed on him, and he was urged to stay with them.

After a time, the Ranger, seated beside Mrs. Garrett, was able to get her to talking. She was willing enough to go over the details of the entire affair, and was instinctively drawn to Hatfield, recognizing him as a friend.

But she could add little to the information the Ranger had already gleaned, though she corroborated all Warden had told him.

The Garretts had surely filed their title properly — yet it was now missing at the Austin land office. Their lawyer had been unable to locate any record to prove the property belonged to Garrett.

"And Frank, yore son — is he with yuh?" asked Hatfield, when Mrs. Garrett had finished.

"He's gone to Austin," she replied. "He's determined to get to the bottom of it all. I wanted him to stay with me but he was so restless, after his father was killed, that he set about solving the mystery himself. I had a letter from him this morning. Frank says he may get a job as a clerk at the General Land Office."

Mrs. Tate called them all into the kitchen to eat then, and they went. The food was excellent and there was plenty of it — fried steak and potatoes, home-made bread and butter, molasses, coffee, baked beans and other foods they enjoyed. The big family and their guests sat around the groaning board, waited on by the Tate girls and Sue. Hatfield aroused the admiration of the other young men by his capacity, though they were champions themselves at the table.

They spent a pleasant evening, and later the Ranger bunked in the shed with Warden and the other cowboys.

Next morning, Warden begged him to stay, at least for a few days.

"I spoke to Tate, Jim," young Warden said. "He says he'll give yuh a job if that's what yuh're huntin'. Hang around a while."

"Thanks a-mighty, Warden, but I got to mosey. I'll be back, though, I reckon. Meanwhile, if yuh don't mind a bit of advice, after this keep yore horse handy while yuh're surveyin'!"

Warden grinned ruefully.

"I shore will," he promised. "They'll have to burn the woods and sift the ashes to catch me again." He rubbed his lean throat speculatively.

Warden rode with Hatfield to a crossroads. A faded wooden sign pointed southeast. "Vanceville," it said, in a lack-lustre way.

"Yuh'll cross E P range if yuh shortcut," informed Warden. "I wouldn't trust none of Pallette's men these days, though, if I was you. He's shore taken a rough bunch."

"Gracias," said Hatfield. "When I finish my business, I'll mebbe come back."

He saluted Warden, and they parted.

CHAPTER V
BIG ED

Crossing the rolling, grassy range, the golden sorrel picked up speed. It was a sunny, fine day, with a gentle breeze from the west. The warm herbage gave off a pleasant scent, and butterflies and birds flitted over the flowers. Cattle grazed in bunches.

Hatfield was planning to stop at Pallette's first, then make for Vanceville, and Warden had told him the location of the E P Ranch. Hatfield knew he had made an enemy of Five-Finger Henny and others of the prize pirate crew which had been placed in charge of the Garrett spread by Pallette, so he intended to approach the E P with due caution, just in case any of the men he had fought against might be there.

Smoke stained the clear blue sky. He could see it before he topped the last wooded rise overlooking the large collection of buildings on the river bank. It was the

E P, a really great spread, with a many-winged ranchhouse, big bunkhouse to accommodate up to fifty punchers; corrals, stables, cribs, and storage sheds. It was from the forge chimney of the blacksmith's shop that the smoke issued.

Ready for anything, the Ranger slowly rode into the yard. In the shade lounged a group of men. They wore the clothing of cowboys, but in no other way did they resemble genuine waddies. And they had the same vicious air as the fellows with whom the Ranger had clashed at the Garrett ranch. They eyed him insolently, but no one attempted to stop him as he strode to the long front veranda.

"Howdy, gents," he said, addressing the two men who were sitting in rocking-chairs on the porch.

"Howdy yoreself," replied one of them, a tall, big-boned fellow.

He was perhaps forty. His black hair was straight, and his dark eyes, with black circles under them, were set deep in a horselike, doleful face. He certainly had a worried look, thought Hatfield, as though much dissatisfied with the way the world was treating him.

His clothing was expensive. His hat was worth seventy-five dollars, perhaps, and his boots were custom-made. Everything he wore had been made from the best materials.

The man beside the horse-faced fellow was stouter, shorter. He wore a "city" suit and white shirt. His hat lay on the porch floor beside him, and Hatfield saw a bald area in his chestnut hair. His nose had been broken, and his eyes were a dark-violet. They were startling in their strange color and piercing gaze.

"Are you Ed Pallette?" Hatfield asked the man who had deigned to greet him.

"That's me," acknowledged Horse-Face.

"I was told I might pick up a ridin' job here. My handle is Hays."

"I see." The tall man nodded. "Yuh can rope, I take it, and savvy the work. Yuh can shore ride, for I watched yuh comin' across the pasture. I could use yuh —" He stopped short as his companion cleared his throat significantly.

"Where are you from?" demanded the man with the gap in his hair, coldly, suspiciously. "Who told you to ask for work here?"

"Why me, I'm from where I come from," Hatfield drawled pleasantly, "and an hombre who met my Dutch uncle in Oscaloosa told my best friend's brother a bird had told him the E P needed riders."

"H'm." The humor did not please the inquisitive man. "You'd be better off to keep a civil tongue in your head." He lapsed into scowling silence.

Big Ed Pallette gulped. "Well, I don't know." He shot a quick sideward glance at his associate.

"If you want my opinion," said that associate, "I say no. He looks like the king of the horsethieves to me."

"Thanks for the boost, mister," said the Ranger.

The man with the bald spot shrugged. He would not rise to bait, and his attitude was hopeless so far as Hatfield went. Pallette shook his head.

"Sorry, big feller," he said. "Season's slack. Try me in the fall."

Hatfield waved a hand, turned the sorrel, and rode around the house.

"Dog it, Vale!" he heard Big Ed Pallette burst out. "That's a good man yuh made me leave go! These cusses you fetched in are the laziest set of dogs I ever hope to —"

Hard eyes were watching from the shade by the bunkhouse and barn, and Hatfield could not linger too long to overhear what was being said around the corner. None of Five-Finger Henny's gang was about the

E P. They were still holding the fort at Garrett's, no doubt.

"Vale has a lot of say with Pallette, but Pallette don't seem to like it too much," Hatfield mused, as he took a trail away from the big ranch, and headed straight for the town.

There wasn't too much to Vanceville. It was a cowtown, serving the ranches of the surrounding country. Like most towns of the Southwest it had a central plaza, planted with live-oaks and other trees, and about this were important buildings such as the city hall and jail. Wooden buildings lined the dusty streets, and Vanceville had more than its quota of saloons. One, the largest and most ornate was the Golden Horns. A gilded set of longhorns overhung the sign over the front door.

It was suppertime, and the Ranger dropped Goldy's reins over the hitch-rack, ducked under it, and went to the bar. Men were in there, drinking. Hatfield had a couple, then went next door to the Texas Lunch, where he ordered ham and eggs, coffee, and apple pie.

Dark fell, as he ate his meal and then rolled a smoke.

Sitting by the front window of the restaurant, drinking his sixth cup of coffee, the Ranger saw Big Ed Pallette and Barney Vale ride up, dismount, and go into the Golden Horns.

They were worth watching, he thought. Warden and the Garretts suspected them of having killed Lew Garrett. Here was a good chance to do a little checking up, so Hatfield paid his bill and went out. When he entered the Golden Horns he was in time to see Vale and Pallette pass through the main bar and enter a hallway at the rear.

After a time, the Ranger went around to the back street. He soon discovered the two men, seated in one of Pallette complaining of Vale's hold over him, had been tantalizing. He would like to sit in on more conversation between those two.

The open window was on a passage between streets. He edged over, trying to get where he could hear what was being said inside.

A low, metallic *cluck-cluck* made him whirl, and drop to the ground instantly.

"Reach!"

A bullet sang over the Ranger's dropping head. A breath later he had made a snap draw and fired into the dark figure of a gunman who was almost upon him.

But this was not the only man near him.

The next instant, in the dim darkness, he made out more men, drawn in his direction by the hubbub. Bodyguards to Vale and Pallette the Ranger believed.

The horse-faced rancher and his companion, inside the private room, leaped up, and drawing guns, rushed to the window. But Hatfield was already streaking toward the sidewalk. Glancing back, he saw men looming in the shaft of light from the open window at which Vale and Pallette stood.

A bullet whizzed near, but he turned the corner, making the front veranda of the saloon. There he paused. Inside, customers were crowding about the bar, and a piano and fiddle were being tortured. Dancers in the side pavilion were shaking the walls and floors as they pranced around.

The Ranger went through the batwings and unobtrusively found a place at the bar. Soon he had a drink. Men were busy with their own devices and in the general confusion had not noticed him.

Big Ed Pallette appeared from the rear, walking fast, followed by two plug-uglies with drawn Colts. The shots which had been fired had attracted little attention, for hilarious cowboys often fired their revolvers into the air in sheer exuberance.

As Pallette and his men passed through

the saloon, a lean, weathered fellow with a faded, string mustache, got up from a poker game and intercepted the rancher near where the Ranger slouched in the crowd at the bar.

"What's wrong, Ed?" demanded the oldish man. Hatfield took note of his worn black pants and run-over boots. "Yuh ain't s'posed to wave guns in here." As he turned a little, Hatfield saw the sheriff's star pinned to the brown vest.

"Oh, hullo, Craig," said Pallette, pausing as the officer seized his arm. "A dry-gulcher just tried for Barney Vale and me through the back winder. We're after him. He run into the street."

"So he's Sheriff Al Craig," mused the Ranger.

Craig had an honest though defeated look. He was a plodder, decided Hatfield, as Craig, his mental processes none too quick, bit at his mustache. Finally he nodded.

"All right," he said wearily. "I'll help yuh hunt him. Come on."

All the searchers rushed outside, splitting up and down the sidewalk, looking for Hatfield, who enjoyed his drink and then had a second, until the chagrined Pallette, Craig and the rest came back and returned to their own pursuits. When Pallette passed,

Hatfield was turned away, his head down, and the tall rancher did not notice him.

A sour, faraway expression was on Pallette's horse face. He seemed to be discussing something unpleasant, most of the time, with some imaginary opponent.

"Austin next," thought Hatfield. "I got to check up on the Land Office records myself, before I go farther."

He had learned what he could in his quick survey, and had many matters to think over. The capital, with its great array of official records representing every square foot in the huge state, called him.

The Garretts were not the sort of folks who would fight the law, and lie. Hatfield was convinced they had been terribly wronged. The Ranger also had decided that Barney Vale was a fishy customer, and he knew that Big Ed Pallette was thick with Vale. As for Sheriff Craig, the lawman might be either a paid or deluded tool of the two. It would not be the first time such officials had been bought by big cowmen.

When all was quiet, Hatfield left the Golden Horns, picked up Goldy, and rode out of Vanceville, taking the trail to Austin. Around midnight, he pulled off the beaten way and camped, to sleep.

When the tall Ranger entered Captain Bill

McDowell's office the next morning — a bright, sunny day — the old Ranger captain looked up in surprise.

"Yuh made it there and back mighty fast," he growled. "Well?"

Hatfield sank into the chair by Cap'n Bill's desk.

"The Garretts got a raw deal, I reckon," he reported. "They lost their land and Lew Garrett was killed — shot down when he tried to do some detective work on his own. Big Ed Pallette, owner of the E P, and a land shark named Barney Vale are mighty busy over there, Cap'n."

"Barney Vale?" repeated McDowell, his frosty brows joined in a scowl. "Why, he's got an office right across from the courthouse, around the corner from the General Land Office!"

Hatfield vigorously nodded assent.

"I got to try and check up at the Land Office. Yuh reckon it would be possible for anybody to steal or switch records there?"

McDowell stared at the blank wall as he thought that over. His gnarled fingers, stiff with his age, drummed on the blotter. At last he looked into the Ranger's gray-green eyes.

"Might be," he muttered. "See here, Jim, I got another one for yuh, like the Garrett business. Come in the mail this mornin', from Kimble County — west of Gillespie, which Vanceville sets in."

He passed the letter to Hatfield who read the painful scrawl which informed:

Sir, Capt. Tex. Rangers. My ranch has bin tuk from me Sherif Lynes says legal like. But I file when I settle 15 yrs. bak. Now Larsen of Tri. 3 brand he adds to Tri. 3. I fite but posse chase me off. Wil Rangers let this happen?

John Porter

"Sounds like the same sort of game," commented the Ranger. "As soon as I finish in town, I'll run over and talk to John Porter."

"*Bueno.* He's asked Ranger help — and we never refuse an appeal from a good citizen. I smell something mighty rotten. We got to dig it out and clean things up."

Hatfield left Cap'n Bill and rode slowly up the street on the golden sorrel, admiring anew this town which he had adopted as his own — as much as he had any town or city. Old Austin drowsed on the north bank of the Colorado River, safe enough on its bluffs from high water when the river flooded.

The roads were dusty now, in the summer

heat. Men sought the shade of the sun awnings, or kept quiet in the saloons, till the noonday passed.

Wooden frame buildings, stores, homes, more pretentious brick and stone edifices made up Austin, named for the father of Texas. There was talk of a new big capitol building for Texas, for the machinery of government was growing more complex in the huge State. But Jim Hatfield loved it as it was.

A great town, Austin, and a great State — Texas.

CHAPTER VI
LAND OFFICE

When Hatfield had first heard Barney Vale's name, it had struck a familiar cord in his mind. Now he was looking for the man's office, and the board sign, hanging in front of a place not far from the courthouse, which would point out Vale's place of business.

He knew that he had seen the land agent's shingle, but was not too familiar with the business places here in the capital, since his work kept him out of town a great deal of the time. Anyway he usually avoided cities as far as possible, preferring the freedom of the wilds.

Finally the sign loomed up ahead of him. It read:

Barney Vale
Land Titles a Specialty
Ranch & Farm Lands for Sale

From his saddle, Hatfield could see through a plate-glass window into the office. A clerk was seated on a stool before a high, slanting desk, writing in a ledger. There was no sign of Vale, but the Ranger had not expected there would be. Hatfield had made a quick run back to Austin, and he doubted if Vale had yet reached town. Probably the land shark was still at Pallette's ranch.

Vale's place was by no means the largest land office in sight. The General Land Office dominated the neighborhood. It stood on a steep hill around the corner from the courthouse. Its thick stone walls looked ancient, venerable — as it should. For the structure was a replica of a medieval European castle.

Leaving Goldy in the shade, Hatfield climbed the stone steps and entered the building. It was cool inside, rather dim, and the air had a papery, musty odor. Offices opened from a central hall. He went to the file room which was marked by a plain painted sign, his spurs clinking softly.

A single door led into the file room which was large, and built much like a vast vault. On shelves reaching to the ceiling and in myriad cubbyholes were millions of records, archives, title deeds, patents, transfers and other legal documents having to do with the ownership of all lands in Texas. The individual files were in paper folders, and listed according to system.

Three clerks were behind a counter, and a slim young man with reddish hair and a thin face was sweeping the floor. At long tables in the space allotted to investigators sat three or four oldish men, in plain clothing. The Ranger recognized a couple of them as Austin attorneys. No doubt, they were studying and searching titles for clients.

Hatfield paused in the doorway as he took in the studious, quiet scene. It did not seem possible that outlawry would dare invade this staid and legal domain.

The youth with the red hair reminded Hatfield of someone he had seen recently. Then he had it.

"Dollars to doughnuts that's Frank Garrett!" he thought. "And he's got a job here, like he hoped he would."

One of the men behind the counter sat at a desk marked "Chief Clerk." He was a small fellow, with a shiny bald pate and sagging cheeks, caused by missing teeth.

Hatfield stepped over to the nearest of the clerks who went on leisurely with what he was doing, writing slowly in a big ledger, engrossed in his task. Hatfield had to rap twice before the man looked up, rather impatiently.

"Yes? What is it?"

"I'd like to see a couple of files, mister," murmured Hatfield.

The clerk rose and came to him, frowning.

"Yuh see about a million. What numbers yuh want?"

"I ain't shore. I'm intersted in Gillespie and Kimble Counties, though. Say the properties of Edward Pallette, of the E P brand, and Larsen of the Triangle Three."

"Yuh're shore green, ain't yuh?" said the clerk, with a veteran's contempt for the uninitiated. "Well, I'm a busy man, but I'll give yuh a hand. First we'll hunt it up in the alphabetical lists and see what files yuh want." He had the average public official's ill-concealed scorn for members of the body politic whose servant he was supposed to be.

"Mighty white of yuh to bother with me, mister," drawled the Ranger. "Yuh savvy a lot more'n I do."

"Naturally." The flattery mollified the clerk and he melted a bit, missing the soft sarcasm.

The red-haired sweeper had paused when he heard the inquiry about the E P. He stared at Hatfield, who was more sure than ever now that the lad was Frank, Sue Garrett's brother.

The clerk hunted up file numbers. He disappeared into the musty stacks, as Hatfield leaned on the counter. Young Garrett watched the tall man curiously.

Hatfield knew that he was on unfamiliar ground. Land titles and such were complicated and it took long experience to understand the problems. But he was seeking an answer to the terrible mystery which had struck the Texas range, and he meant to learn all he could.

The clerk brought various records in paper wrappers.

"Yuh can take these to the table and study 'em, but don't remove 'em from the office," said the clerk, self-importantly.

"Thanks a-mighty."

The Ranger went to a vacant table and sat down. The rough processes of land ownership were known to Hatfield, but he quickly learned that it took an expert to know exactly what was required in proving a title at law. There were many entries in the long records, sales, new owners, complex procedures which must be traced.

He felt decidedly at sea. But after a time he was able to locate lines recording Ed

Pallette's title deeds.

"Well, dog my hide!" he murmured.

Pallette held a great sweep of land across Gillespie, but the record showed it was jointly owned by Barney Vale. If anything happened to one or the other owner, the survivor became sole holder!

"Pallette and Vale seem to be close pardners," he thought. "Or mebbe Pallette don't savvy this."

The Ranger kept on searching, but was unable to turn up the slightest evidence to show that Lewis Garrett had ever held any land in the district.

It was puzzling. He tried another file which the clerk searched out for him. It contained what seemed to be iron-clad records proving that Benjamin Larsen of the Triangle 3 — and here a new name, Samuel Ince, entered the perplexing picture — owned with Ince a large chunk of Kimble County.

John Porter, whose pitiful complaint had reached McDowell, did not appear in the records. If Garrett and Porter had actually been owners of Texas ground, their deeds would have been recorded and properly filed at the Land Office. But if there had been errors of filing, then the tracts would class as unappropriated public domain, open to location. Hatfield was aware that title defects could wreck a claim.

"Garrett and Porter may have been careless in how they registered," he thought.

As for old Possum Ransom, such a squatter had not a leg to stand on. He had not filed, and, as land increased in value, others coveted it, and it was vital to hold a clean title.

"Wonder who Samuel Ince is?" Hatfield asked himself.

It seemed to him something more than coincidence that this Ince should be on the file with Larsen, in the same capacity as Vale and Pallette.

He studied the papers on which the records were inscribed and thought it seemed old enough for the dates. And the phrasing was stiff, and sounded quite legal. Hatfield was no lawyer, to find flaws, but he doubted if there were any. Even the ink was black, well-dried.

Such a man as Barney Vale, he thought, might seize opportunities to shove out small holders of land, who had filed improperly. But Vale would be way ahead of him, knowing every wrinkle, every necessary twist to cinch ownership in a court. It took years of intense study to grow familiar with the complexities of the Land Office.

Hatfield found that he had spent over an hour studying the files. The air was stale, musty in there. He returned the files, and went out into the street. The fresh air, hot as it was, smelled delicious after the confined atmosphere of the Land Office.

The Ranger had a drink, then went to McDowell's office.

"Find anything?" inquired the old Captain.

"I don't know, suh. I savvy one thing, though. It takes a real expert to understand all the wrinkles at that place."

"Barney Vale's been around Texas a long while," observed Captain Bill. "Such an hombre has vast knowledge of how to locate surveys, and how to smell out defects in a title."

"Right," agreed Jim Hatfield. "And it looks to me like Vale has fixed hisself up fine. He's joint owner of Pallette's E P. Looks like him and Pallette are in thick together on a big deal." Hatfield spoke morosely, for he was finding difficulty in getting started on the case. He could not yet see the road ahead. "I better head for Kimble County, Cap'n, and talk to John Porter, check up on Larsen's Triangle Three, and some hombre who's joint owner with Larson, name of Sam Ince."

The Ranger took his leave of McDowell and once more set out westward. The roads he followed were of dirt. When he had left the city behind, they petered out. They were fit enough for horses, but carts had rutted the soil and there was no real highway for wheeled vehicles.

He had plenty to think about, as he tried to figure out the puzzles he had encountered at the Land Office. . . .

In the evening, two days later, Hatfield located John Porter at the address given in Porter's letter to the Rangers. Porter was a thick-set, middle-aged Texan. He was working on a ranch not far from the little settlement of Beansboro, in Kimble County.

Porter had ridden up to the boardinghouse where Hatfield was staying for Porter wanted to be near his daughters, who were working in the town. The Ranger had been waiting for him. Hatfield had told Porter that McDowell had asked him to check up on the complaint the Rangers had received.

Porter accompanied Hatfield to a nearby saloon, and over drinks it was easy to start the rancher talking. The Ranger wanted to know all there was to know about the man.

John Porter, he learned, was a widower, with three grown girls. His children had helped on the little ranch, several miles from

Beansboro, until they had been dispossessed by Sheriff Lynes and a posse. Then the girls had gone to work as waitresses in the settlement.

Porter had a deep sense of grievance, as well he might have. For he was a plodding, peaceful citizen.

"I'm no gunslinger," he told Hatfield, "and Sheriff Lynes said this Sam Ince and Ben Larsen of the Triangle Three had me on the fork and over the fire toastin'. I asked a friend of mine in town who does some law work about it. He told me I couldn't win, and I ain't got the money to hire lawyers and take it through the courts anyways. I was licked before I begun."

"Is this Sheriff Lynes honest?" asked the Ranger.

"Far as I savvy. He seemed to feel sorry for us, but said he had to carry out the law."

"Yuh shore yuh filed proper-like on yore land?"

"Positive, mister. I'd swear to it if it cost me my neck. But things were all wrong in Austin at the Land Office, 'cordin' to what I learned."

"And this here Ince? Yuh say him and Larsen took yore place?"

"Yeah. Ince was a stranger. He come here when they started makin' me all that

74

trouble. He seems to be in cahoots with Larsen, who was mighty glad to see me go. I had some fences which bothered the Triangle Three. I savvy that Larsen claimed some squatter land, too, and run folks off that was on it."

The situation was parallel to that in Gillespie County. But unlike Lew Garrett, Porter had not tried to buck the enemy, and perhaps had saved his life by accepting the injustice.

"I'll be headin' for Austin soon, Porter, and I'll shore tell McDowell how things stand here," promised Hatfield. "Meanwhile, make no move, savvy? Make out like yuh've swallered it and are satisfied."

"Aw right," said Porter and, as he glanced up, he suddenly caught the Ranger's arm. "Say, there's Larsen now!"

Hatfield turned to look at the tall, tow-headed man in leather and big Stetson who swaggered into the saloon. Ben Larsen, owner of the Triangle Three, a big spread, wore a mustache and clipped beard of light hue like his ropy hair.

"Drinks are on the Triangle Three, gents!" he roared. "Step up!"

"That's Sam Ince with him," growled Porter.

Ince was a shorter, heavier man. He wore

a rusty black and a hand hat. He had a fleshy face that was blue around the jowls, and his eyes were too small and too closely set together.

"I'll go over and have a look-see," the Ranger told Porter. "Remember what I said — keep yore temper and don't go off half-cocked. Yuh'll hear further from the Rangers, savvy?"

For John Porter, at sight of the men who had snatched away the little home he had worked for, had grown as mad as fire. His fists clenched, and he scowled at Ben Larsen and Sam Ince.

"All right," he choked to the Ranger. "I'll keep my trap shut. But I can't stand the smell of 'em. See yuh again."

John Porter jumped up and hurried outside.

Hatfield pushed to the bar, to take advantage of the rancher's offer to free drinks. He managed to edge in close to Larsen and Ince where he could listen to what they said.

Ince, the pig-faced man, was apparently about to take his leave, for a time, anyway.

"I've got to start, Larsen," he was saying. "See you in a few days."

"Right, right." Larsen was grinning. He was in an expansive mood. "Here's to luck!

Everything's worked out plumb fine."

Ince had several drinks before he shook hands with Larsen and stalked out. His step was unsteady by that time, for he was filled with red-eye. His saddled horse waited with reins over the long rail. Ince managed to mount, and started away.

Hatfield followed, at a safe distance. He wanted to know where Ince was going.

In the darkness, the Ranger could sniff the freshly risen dust kicked up by Ince's plodding horse. Ince was half numb from the liquor he had consumed, and as his mustang climbed a hill, the stubby figure was framed against the moon. Ince had no suspicion that he was followed.

Chapter VII
Tiger Bait

It was nearly midnight when Sam Ince rode up to Big Ed Pallette's ranchhouse, dropped his reins, and walked stiffly toward the front. There was a lamp burning in the main room, and Ince entered.

Hatfield stealing through the shadows came up under an open window. Barney Vale sat in the big room. Pallette was there, too, but Big Ed was slumped, snoring, in a chair. An empty bottle was at his limp hand which sagged to the floor.

Ince glanced at Pallette as he blinked in the yellow light.

"He's out completely," growled Barney Vale. His eyes glowed. He had been drinking, but he held his liquor well. "Everything all right over there, Ince?"

"Yes, suh. John Porter made no trouble to speak of, and we run off the squatters. I got held up, though, by them Olsen brothers. They opened fire on Lynes' posse and we had quite a chase. Wounded one and run 'em into the chaparral."

"The fools! They've got no chance."

"That's what we told 'em but they're hot-headed cusses. Yuh want me to move on west?"

"Wait a while," said Vale. "I'll tell you when. There's a job here in Gillespie. I've been puttin' it off, but it's got to be done."

"Yuh mean Tate's?" Ince blinked harder.

"That's it. The Garretts are there. But we've got to clear the place out. I may use you. It'll be up to that old fool Al Craig this time."

"And you?" asked Ince. "You stickin' here?"

Vale shook his head. He looked sinister as he crouched in his chair.

"I'm going to Austin for a few days," he said. "Then I'll be back. Let you know in the morning what to do."

"That suits me," Sam Ince answered as he yawned. "I'm plumb wore out, boss. Reckon I'll turn in."

Ince walked through to the interior of the great house.

Barney Vale sat still, staring at the opposite wall. His eyes had a cold marblelike glint. He reached out, poured himself several fingers of whisky, downed it at a gulp. . . .

In the bright morning, on the run to Austin ahead of Barney Vale, Jim Hatfield had been riding some hours when he lifted his head and sniffed at the risen dust before him. He could see a long, rolling cloud of the reddish stuff hanging in the quiet air, moving slowly eastward toward the capital.

"Trail herd, Goldy," he murmured to the sorrel.

The signs he had already cut were as plain as a printed page to him — the chopped earth, the hoofmarks of longhorn cattle, and of horses ridden by the drovers. The criss-crossing, snakelike marks off to one side showed where the chuckwagon had passed, driven by cookie.

Those cattle were being driven to Austin, Hatfield knew for the capital was an important market for livestock, as well as for cotton, grain and wool. It was the principal trade and jobbing center for central Texas. Cattle herds were often driven to the city, and it was no surprise to cut such a trail. With such a slow party, though, it would be another day before they finished the drive.

Coming up the next rise, Hatfield could see the drag riders moving in dense dust. Now and then it shut them off from his vision. The wagon had gone on ahead to the next bedding-ground.

Hatfield observed his usual caution in catching up with the cattle drive. Not only for his own sake, but he did not wish to start a stampede, as trail cattle were apt to prove spooky.

A small bunch of big steers broke off from one side of the herd, and a flanker spurted out to head them back into line. The longhorns came close enough so the Ranger was able to make out the brand. It was a Lazy J — and Hatfield nodded his satisfaction, for he knew the outfit and its owner, Jake Jervis. The ranch lay east of the Pecos, near the Edwards Plateau, and was a large one.

The previous year, the Ranger had smashed an outlaw gang which had been preying on Jervis and others near the Pecos. Now Jervis was a sworn friend of Hatfield and of the Texas Rangers.

Jim Hatfield rode nearer now, and waved to the dragmen. One of them recognized him, and pointed up ahead.

"Boss is up at point," he signaled.

Hatfield allowed plenty of room and moved so as not to alarm the steers, plodding toward their fate — beefsteaks for the tables of city homes and restaurants.

When he rose up to the front of the long procession, he had his bandanna raised to sift some of the dust. He still was coughing and sniffing from the clinging, powdery stuff that clung to his throat and nostrils.

Jake Jervis waved and grinned at him. The Ranger joined the owner of the herd.

Jervis was a tall, light-haired Texan, of about forty. He had lobster-red skin, and a loud voice. He was glad to see Hatfield, profane in his cheery greeting.

"You old seacook!" he cried. "I was hopin' I'd run into yuh. Here, have a swig as a starter."

He passed over a flask of whisky, and the Ranger took a drink.

Jervis drank also, and smacked his lips.

"Whew! Been a dusty drive. Rivers are down, though — that's a comfort. Ain't had any bad swims."

"How are things at the Lazy J?" asked the Ranger.

"Fine, fine," replied Jervis. "In the pink, as them English fellers say, and gettin' redder all the time. You chasin' bandits?"

"I'm tryin' to make shore just what I am chasin this time," Hatfield said drily. "By the way, yuh havin' any squatter trouble, Jake?"

Jervis swore with sulphurous, picturesque phrases.

"Cuss 'em! Always squatters, movin' in on a man. Shore I've got trouble with 'em.

Who ain't — in this business?"

The Ranger rode for a time at point with the boss of the Lazy J. Business was good, the price of beef was up, and Jervis had just become the proud father of twin boys.

"I've got to be moseyin' on, Jake," Hatfield finally said. "I've got business, and yuh're movin' a little too slow for me. Where yuh stoppin' in town?"

"At the Drovers' Inn, of course. And if yuh don't drop in and help me drink the bar dry, I'll never forgive the Rangers!"

The germ of an idea had struck Hatfield, as he paused a moment, just before he gave Goldy his head. "Ever act as tiger bait, Jake?" he asked.

"Huh?" Jervis's good-humored red face went blank. "What's the game, Ranger?"

"I might ask yuh to give me a hand in Austin, if things work out like I'm hopin'."

"Say, any time, any time at all," Jervis said heartily. "You savvy that. Don't forget, now — at the Drovers', and we'll be in by to-morrer night."

Late that afternoon, Captain Bill McDowell listened to Hatfield's report on the complaint from John Porter.

"And now?" inquired McDowell, brows knitted.

"Barney Vale's on his way to Austin,

Cap'n," informed the tall Ranger. "I'm goin' after him, though I ain't shore yet just how he's workin' his game."

"All right." There was a keen light in Mc-Dowell's blue eyes. He licked his cracked lips, as though in anticipation. "I can't ride far, mebbe, Hatfield, but if it comes to it, here in Austin — well, I ain't had any real sport for a long time."

He opened the drawer under his hand and drew forth his Colt .45 Frontier Model pistol. It was well-oiled and in perfect shape, and McDowell ran his hand along it proudly.

"I want to be in on anything that breaks loose in town, savvy?" he said. "That is, if it ain't hamperin' you."

Hatfield smiled.

"Shore," he said, for he knew the pent-up emotions of the old warhorse, Bill McDowell, chained to his desk by the infirmities consequent on long decades of life. . . .

Barney Vale, accompanied by several riders, reached town after dark that night. He went to his office for a time, then repaired to a hotel to eat and drink. Hatfield observed the land agent from a distance. He did not wish to alarm Vale.

The stout agent worked at his office the following day. In the afternoon, Jake Jervis, trailed by some of his men, arrived at the Drover's Inn. The cows had been penned on the outskirts of the city, and Jervis, his long run ended, was ready for sport.

The Ranger did not immediately seek out the rancher, who was his staunch friend, but waited, giving Jervis time to eat and have a few drinks before sending a note into him by a boy. On reading it, Jervis left his own companions and came to the rear of the inn. He found Hatfield awaiting him in a small private room. A bottle and glasses were on the table there.

"Drink up, Jake," invited the Ranger. "I want to talk."

"Well, why all the mystery? Yuh ashamed to be seen with me in public?" Jervis grinned. "Here, the cigars are on me — for the twins. I had to wait till I hit town to buy enough to go around."

Over the cigars and whisky, Hatfield broached the subject he had in mind.

"I'm on the trail of a land shark named Barney Vale," he explained. "He has an office here but he's operatin' west of Austin at the moment. He's hoggin' big stretches, and runnin' off small landholders and squatters. It looks legal — on paper. I believe Vale's a thief and worse, but I've got to prove it to the hilt. You can help us."

85

"Anything at all," said Jervis. "I said that, and I mean it, Ranger!"

"In the mornin' then" — Hatfield became businesslike — "send a message to Vale that yuh want to talk with him. Make it here in this room. I'll be behind that closet door, where I can get a look and listen. I need to make shore how Vale works, savvy? Be friendly with Vale. Tell him yuh heard from a pard of Big Ed Pallette's — he owns the E P in Gillespie County — that Vale might be able to give yuh a hand. Yuh got plenty troubles. Squatters and settlers have fenced in yore water and cut off yore range and yuh want 'em cleaned off, yuh don't care how. If Vale asks for money, give him this hundred dollars to start."

Jervis pushed away the roll which Hatfield offered.

"I'll put up the stake myself if necessary," he said, his jaw set with determination. . . .

Barney Vale stepped into the private room at the Drovers' Inn.

"You're Jake Jervis?" he said to the man who was waiting there.

"Yes, suh. Take it yuh're Barney Vale?" Jervis was friendly, pleasant. "Sit down and take the load off yore feet. Have a drink."

Inside the closet, Hatfield sat on a soap box, his eye to a crack. He could see Vale's

86

stout figure and the man's cruel face. As Vale removed his hat and sat down opposite Jervis, the bald spot gleamed in the sunlight coming through the window. The agent's violet eyes were fixed on Jervis's lobster-red face, as Vale studied the rancher.

Jervis did a good job. He poured a drink for Vale and himself, offered two cigars, one for each twin. He swore in his hearty fashion, and began his tale of woe.

"Run into Marty Dugan a while back Vale," he said. "I was tellin' him what a fuss I had with all-fired farmers and small-timers comin' in on my range."

"You own the Lazy J," said Vale. "I know the property."

So he had looked Vale up, thought Hatfield, and was glad he had picked a bona-fide candidate to draw out the land shark.

A shadow touched the wall outside the room, the elongated shadow of a Stetson, the vague outline of a man's body. Hatfield was not surprised. Vale seldom took chances. He had a bodyguard, wherever he moved.

"That's right," Jervis was saying. "Dugan's a friend of Ed Pallette's, and when he was cussin' squatters and all, Dugan said he'd heard that the E P had had the same trouble and that mebbe you could help me out. I'm willin' to pay, of course. I can't run the cows I did, with my water bein' cut off by fences and all."

"You have the same problem as most big cowmen, Jervis," Vale replied. "You can't possibly buy up all the range you need, and these little fellows take up title and wreck you. Yes, you came to the right man. I'll need some details — and a deposit, of course, say one hundred and fifty dollars."

The roll which Jervis instantly pulled from his pocket was large enough to choke a bull. It made Vale regretful he had not asked for more. Jervis peeled off three fifties. He held the money in his hand as he spoke.

"How you aim to clean off them skunks, Vale?" he asked. "I savvy for a fact that a couple got legal titles to the chunks of land they're livin' on."

"Which ones?" Vale asked quickly.

"Well, Greene Tillsbury, for one, and for another, a Mexican named Diaz."

Vale made notes.

"Don't worry about it any more, Jervis," he said expansively. "I'll see to everything for you."

Jervis was reluctant to pass over the cash deposit. He frowned.

"How do I know yuh'll be able to?" he asked. "I don't see how yuh can hope to bust their holds on their property."

Vale shrugged. His eyes were cold.

"I'll guarantee you satisfaction or your money back, Jervis. As to how I'll handle it, that's my business. I have influence, though. I'll say that."

Hatfield watched the scene as the rancher drew Vale out, doing a fine job of acting. Jervis feigned to be convinced against his will, and gave Vale the money.

"I'll go over the matter as soon as possible," Vale said. "I've been mighty busy lately. I'll let you know what the job will cost in the long run. Wait till you hear from me, before you take any further action, understand?"

"I savvy. Thanks a mighty." Jervis acted relieved.

CHAPTER VIII
CORNERED

Vale had another drink, then rose, shook hands, and departed. The shadow of the sentry on the wall outside left with the land shark.

Most thieves, thought Hatfield, had a system. It worked once, twice, and they counted on it working indefinitely. He hoped Barney Vale would follow the rule, and so give some idea of his mode of operation.

He took his leave of Jake Jervis, and left the Drovers' Inn by a rear door.

That afternoon, he watched Barney Vale climb the stone stairs to the General Land Office. Two armed men were tagging along with Vale. They were the same two men the Ranger had seen at the E P when he had been eavesdropping at Pallette's ranch-house. The bodyguards went inside with Vale, and Hatfield moved around to a side entry, keeping out of their sight as they entered the file room.

Frank Garrett was inside, sorting papers at a desk. The chief clerk and the other workers were occupied with routine matters. Vale went to the counter, asked for a file. Hatfield was sure he had asked for a file of the county in which Jervis's Lazy J lay.

Garrett was dog-eyeing Vale, whom he knew, and Vale did not fail to recognize the young man. But the land shark kept his aplomb. He took the file folder, went to a table and sat down, studying it for a time. Young Garrett kept watching Vale steadily.

"Cuss it, Garrett's wreckin' Vale's game — and mine, too," thought the Ranger. "Vale couldn't do anything if he meant to, with Garrett spyin'."

The young waddy was a rank amateur at such work. And he could not help showing that hatred for Vale, who had helped take his father's ranch, and who was suspected of killing Lew Garrett, burned in his heart.

After a while, Vale returned the file, and left. He went back to his office. He had made some notes as he read, but had done nothing illegal.

The patient Ranger bided his time, observing Barney Vale. Such work was often tiresome, but it was also necessary. Vale kept busy in his office for a while, then went out to eat, but soon returned. A client or two came and went.

From the high window of a small saloon across the way, Hatfield saw a hurrying figure reach Vale's office and rush inside. Barney Vale was at a large desk by his window. Hatfield, craning his neck, saw that Vale had been given a letter, which the land agent read, then crunched up and threw to the floor as he leaped to his feet.

Vale started to leave, but went back, picked up the letter, and stuffed it in a pocket. Apparently he was greatly disturbed.

The sun was nearly gone, the shadows long over Austin when Barney Vale, tagged by his guards, went up the sidewalk, and turned into a restaurant. As he ate his dinner there, dark fell over Austin.

Yellow glows came from the windows of buildings as oil lamps were lighted in the city. Tired workers were repairing to their homes or to the bars and other places of amusement. All houses looked cozy after dark, mused the Ranger, as he lurked across the road, waiting for Vale to come out of the restaurant.

But Vale, seated at a round table in the barroom restaurant, appeared to be in no hurry to leave. He was drinking with his friends. Hatfield had time to snatch a sandwich and a drink nearby. Through the window of the place he could watch the building where Vale sat at a table.

Finally Vale decided to return to his office, and the armed men went with him. As Vale lighted a lamp on his desk, a tower clock slowly chimed ten.

People in their houses were beginning to turn in, although there were plenty of celebrants in saloons and other spots who had no such intention. Hatfield stood leaning wearily against a brick wall in a recess across the road. The lamp in Vale's office burned low.

Then he saw the land shark coming from the doorway, and perked up. Shadows marked the bodyguards following their chief, but now there were more than two. At least half a dozen walked in pairs after Barney Vale. Lights from windows glinted on their holstered guns.

This time Vale turned toward the hill on which the Land Office stood. The castle stood out black, with its rococo turrets against the sky.

"He's on his way!" thought the Ranger hopefully. "Mebbe Jervis gave me a real boost!"

Hatfield was careful. He did not wish to

alarm the man he was shadowing. He held back, waiting until all the gang had moved well around the corner. Then he moved, lithely, through the shadows. He paused where he could see the black blobs that were Vale and his men going up the stone steps toward the Land Office.

Suddenly the Ranger tensed, swore under his breath. He saw two more figures pass in the faint shaft from a street light around the corner. He had but a fleeting glimpse, but in that instant saw that one of them was Keith Warden.

"I'll lay anything the other's Frank Garrett!" he thought.

He lost them in the darkness, for they were well ahead, and moving fast. He could not see them on the stairs.

"Warden must have come to Austin to help Frank Garrett buck Barney Vale," he decided. "I've got to warn 'em."

Vale and his cohorts were in deadly earnest. They were killers of the most brutal variety. And the Ranger knew that if he had spied the two young waddies dogging the land agent that there was an excellent chance that Vale's keen-eyed, suspicious gunnies had also glimpsed the pair.

Hatfield did not see Garrett and Warden on the main stairs to the Land Office. The

Ranger waited, but was unable to pick out their shadowy forms.

He began to circle toward the shadowed side of the steep hill. He was worried about Warden and Garrett. He liked Keith Warden, knew how much the cowboy meant to Sue Garrett, and Frank's mother had had enough to bear, without losing her only son.

The Ranger peered into the blackness, and swept the pale moonlit areas.

The warm summer night was fraught with weighted danger. It was like waiting for some buried, murderous explosive to go off, and Hatfield did not know just where that would occur. . . .

Keith Warden lay flat on his stomach. Within a yard of him was Sue's brother, Frank, the slim, red-haired young cowboy who had come to the capital in a desperate effort to retrieve the fortunes of the family, land which had been wrested from them.

Warden felt Frank's light touch on his wrist. He moved his head closer to Garrett's lips.

"Can yuh see 'em?" Frank breathed.

"No. They're up there, though."

"Want to catch Vale right in the act, inside the file room," muttered Frank. "Let's creep a bit nearer."

They inched up the slope. Warden's body

was scraped by gravel, dug into by protruding rocks. In order to crawl noiselessly, the young fellows had taken off their heavy boots, and left their cartridge belts behind. But each had a Colt six-shooter, with some spare shells they had thrust into the pockets of their trousers.

As Ranger Hatfield had surmised, Keith Warden had come to Austin to aid Garrett. Frank had written him, asking him to hurry to the capital, in the hope of trapping and arresting Barney Vale.

Young Garrett, employed at the Land Office, had rented a small furnished room on the north side of town. The landlady had agreed to let Frank's friend stay with him for a time. With Barney Vale in town, Frank could not work all day and watch his enemy all night, so Warden had slept while Frank was at the office.

Barney Vale had visited the Land Office that afternoon, and studied two files in the file room, as the system permitted anyone to do. Frank Garrett had watched the land shark, and he had had a hunch that Vale meant to return after dark.

Keith Warden had willingly accompanied Frank, and they had followed Vale to the Land Office.

Creeping up the slope, they were but a

few yards from the massive, towering walls when they heard a faint metallic click. It was the familiar, recognizable noise made by a squeaky hinge. Garrett gripped Warden's arm in subdued excitement.

"That's Vale! He's got a key to the side door, Keith!"

Frank Garrett was acquainted with the building and the grounds. It was for the purpose of learning the system in use in the Land Office, and figuring out how Barney Vale had managed to steal their ranch, that Frank had taken the job he now held. He expected to be able to expose Vale and regain the Garrett lands, once he had his evidence.

Warden was heart and soul with the Garretts. He was deeply in love with Sue, and looked on Frank as a brother. Besides the injustice he had seen done, he had become personally involved. Vale's men had come within a hair of lynching *him.*

As a rule, Keith Warden, like most young fellows, enjoyed excitement, but now as he hugged the warm dirt he felt an unpleasant sensation in the pit of his stomach. He could not glimpse any of the dangerous foes he and Frank had trailed through the streets, so perhaps it was instinct which was warning him. It was hard to keep patient, not to jump up and charge in blindly, no matter what.

After the click of the lock, the opening of the side door, all was silent — too quiet, thought Warden. From below came noises of the city, distant strains of music, voices raised now and then, but the Land Office brooded in majestic stillness on its hilltop.

Frank Garrett was younger than Keith Warden, and he also was reckless by nature. He had the teenager's superb belief in himself, certain that though others might die, he was sure to survive. He had not lived long enough, nor did he have sufficient experience to realize that he, too, was only mortal. He knew only that he was excited, wrought up, because at last he was closing in on his foe, Barney Vale.

The dark shadow of the wall cloaked the two young men. There were niches and flagged terraces, plenty of spots around the building which would hide men, they saw, as their young eyes sought to pierce the blackness.

Frank Garrett was slithering along, headed toward the side entrance from which they had caught the noises. Keith followed him. Both men were sure that Vale must be inside the file room by this time.

They were nearly up to the granite flagstones outside the door when a sharp, but low voice suddenly said:

"Freeze where yuh are or I'll drill yuh!"

Warden's heart gave a convulsive leap. He was looking toward the spot from which the command had come, and he saw the gleam of eyes, eyes which no doubt had been watching Frank and himself as they approached.

He sensed other enemies at his right.

"Who is it, Gus?" a hoarse whisper inquired.

"One of 'em's Garrett, the young fool who works in the office. I ain't shore of the other. Lucky I spied the cusses trailin' the boss. Stand up, both of yuh, and watch how you move! Savvy?"

Keith Warden was desperate. He had promised Sue and her mother that he would not let anything happen to Frank, and now he and Frank were both prisoners of Barney Vale's. They knew too much to be spared, and Warden was aware of Vale's ruthlessness.

When Frank had called him to Austin, the idea of trailing and trapping Vale had seemed entirely feasible, and success probable. Now Warden saw what a perilous undertaking it actually was, and the bubble of hope in his heart burst.

There was a violent scrabbling sound close to him. He had been momentarily stunned at being captured and under enemy guns. But now he realized that Frank was rolling off, and he immediately followed.

The Vale man fired hastily. The slug plugged into the ground between the two young fellows. Garrett and Warden let go with their six-shooters, and the pistols flamed in the night. Warden jumped up and ran. Garrett was already running full-tilt along the building. Both shot back as they ran, and four or five of their enemies tried for them.

They raced close to a flagged terrace, with a low parapet running around three sides, the rear being a wall of the Land Office.

"In here!" gasped Garrett, as a bullet shrieked within inches of their heads.

Garrett jumped the barrier, fell flat, and Warden nearly fell. As he slowed in recovering, he was framed against the moonlit sky and something tore at his flesh, shocking him from head to toe. He cried out involuntarily, went down. He was stunned, bruised by the fall to the stones, and was yelling, although he hardly knew it. The world whirled about him as he tried to keep his grip on life. He lay with his legs across the parapet, his breath burning his throat.

Frank hastily pulled him in.

"You hit?" he cried, his voice falsetto with alarm.

"Not — too bad!"

It was difficult to speak.

Slugs spattered at them, as Vale's killers closed in. Garrett tugged at Warden's clothing.

"Roll over here, pronto!" Frank ordered vibrantly. "Keep close to the railin'!"

Determined, vicious enemies drove at them, guns blaring.

Chapter IX
The Law's Coming

Jim Hatfield had circled to the shadowed side of the steep hill and started to climb. He had almost reached the summit when revolvers began to blast away, near the front of the Land Office. Men were cursing, and someone — he thought it sounded like Keith Warden — was yelling in pain.

A dark shadow flashed past, running around the Land Office, but whoever it was did not see him. The man was too intent on whatever he was seeking to accomplish to note the silent, prostrate Ranger.

But with the battle opening, Hatfield had thrown caution to the winds. He had a Colt in his hand, the hammer spur back under his thumb. Jumping up, he charged the remaining yards to the hilltop. As he rushed toward the center of the disturbance, he hoped he was not too late!

Reaching the limit of the black shadows cast by the venerable castle walls, Jim Hatfield checked his speed. He did not like the idea of dashing out into that comparatively light area where the moon's rays touched. The building had many turrets and spires, and there were niches and terraces as well, and men could be in ambush in any one of them.

Guns were flaming not far from the front entrance to the Land Office. Hatfield moved in, seeking to determine just what was going on, though he believed Garrett and Warden had found themselves in hot water all right.

He saw a flagged terrace with a low parapet around three sides, its fourth being a wall. Two pistols were snarling from narrow gaps in the sawtooth rampart of the terrace, as men snugged against the front barrier fought for their lives.

Not more than a dozen paces from where the Ranger paused was a dark figure. Hatfield believed it must be the fellow who had run around the building, past him, a few moments before. The gunslinger's back was to the Ranger, and Vale's aide was protected from the terrace field of fire by the sharp corner behind which he was crouching.

On past the terrace where the two victims were lying, were pillars and bulges in the walls, which gave good cover to other gunhands as they poured lead into the flagged terrace.

There was no doubt now in Hatfield's mind that Keith Warden and Frank Garrett were the victims who were trapped on the terrace. The rest of the banging revolvers must be in the hands of Vale's killers, who were trying to get the embattled waddies.

Warden was shouting at the top of his voice. He was telling the drygulching killers what he thought of them, and there was real anguish in his tone of voice. Bullets smashed against granite, causing a rain of metal and rock fragments to fly through the air. Those Warden and Garrett sent back shrieked out over the city, or ploughed into the hill.

The Vale gunslinger nearest Hatfield, intent on killing the luckless youths snuggled in the protection of the parapet, had a bright idea. He could not get quite enough elevation to make his shots, but the corner was formed by serrated granite blocks which made a rough ladder, and the marksman began to climb. He needed only to get up a couple of rungs to have a clear bead on the two victims. Holding on with his left hand, his booted toes in the niches, he took careful aim.

At such range it would be sure death and Warden and Garrett were chiefly occupied with the main gang behind the pillars on the other side of them. Plainly the Vale man the Ranger had seen run around the building had meant to catch them here.

"Now or never!" thought Hatfield, and at that moment he recognized the killer. He was Five-Finger Henny, whom the Ranger had encountered at the Garrett spread.

Hatfield raised his thumb from the hammer spur of his steady, well-aimed Colt, and the gun kick was absorbed by the Ranger's palm. Five-Finger Henny, the Vale henchman, flattened against the stone wall. He flexed, gave an unearthly screech, and fell to the earth by the corner.

It saved the two on the terrace, for the moment. Hatfield hastily rushed to check the prostrate killer. He kicked the fellow's gun away from the limp hand, and crouched there.

The din was frightful. It would be heard in the city below, and Austin had city police, marshals who patrolled the streets. They would hurry to the Land Office to see what was going on, but it would take them a few minutes to reach the place.

Vale's followers realized this, too.

"Rush the cusses, boys!" one of them shouted. "They're out of ammunition!"

Dark figures leaped from behind stone pillars, blasting furiously at Garrett and Warden, who fired only one time more apiece. Evidently the killer's estimation of the situation had been correct. They were short of bullets.

They would have died in the charge had the Ranger not been there. Hatfield let go with all he had. He hit another Vale gun guard who threw up his hands, fell, then rolled over and came up, to limp away. The others were suddenly aware of the deadly fire from the corner, and they swerved. Rapidly the Ranger pumped .45 slugs at the moving, elusive targets. They tried to cow him by hasty shots, but he was protected by the wall corner. Then they broke and ran back to the cover of the porch pillars.

The Vale men stopped, and Hatfield held his fire. There was a brief lull, and the Ranger heard a gruff voice calling:

"Barney, Barney! Watch it, the law's comin'!"

The warning echoed in the deep recesses of the Land Office.

"Hey, up there, what's goin' on!"

A stentorian shout came from the street below, and a couple of city marshals, guns out, started up the stairs.

Vale's men evaporated. Hatfield glimpsed a scurrying figure as one of them galloped around the far side of the Land Office.

"Warden — Garrett!" called the Ranger. "I'm Jim Hays! Hold yore fire! I'm comin' around the mountain!"

Hatfield ran lightly toward the front entrance. He had to pass the flagged terrace, and there lay Frank Garrett and Keith Warden. Warden knew him, recognized the tall figure in the faint light.

"Jim! How — how'd you come here? Was that you saved our hides just now? No need to tell us not to fire. We're out of bullets!"

Frank Garrett was silent, his thin face pale. Specks of blood showed where flying lead and gravel had cut him. Warden was lying on his side.

"Are yuh hit bad, Warden?" asked Hatfield.

"No. They got me through the left shoulder. Aches now — numbness is workin' out."

"Stay where yuh are," Hatfield said quickly. "The police are comin' and might pick yuh off if yuh move. I'm goin' on and try to round up some of them gunfighters of Vale's."

He flashed on, Colt up, searching for enemies in the shadows. As he reached the first stone pillar looming near the entry, he could see that the front door stood ajar.

Behind him, the two marshals had a glimpse of him and yelled to him to halt. As he moved toward the open door, one fired a warning shot which smashed against the pillar and rained fragments down on him.

Hatfield hurried through, kicked the door all the way open and ran inside.

In the dark, spacious hall he could see little, for not much light came in from outside. The file room stood to his right. He heard a sound there, the creak of an un-oiled hinge, and started toward the noise, although it was utterly black over there.

A gun flamed and he felt the singe of the heavy bullet past his cheek. He reacted with lightning speed, throwing himself to one knee, returning the fire.

Somebody was running along the corridor toward the rear of the building. Hatfield jumped up, to follow.

He could hear the marshals yelling out-side, and the voices of Warden and Garrett calling back.

As he galloped along the corridor to the interior of the big structure, another big chunk of lead missed him by only inches, and he placed the man who shot by the flare from the pistol. He tried to down his man but the hall ahead loomed black. Then as the echoes of the explosions died away, he no longer heard the footsteps.

Gun up, the Ranger came to a turn-off, a side corridor which led to a small door. Heavy bar bolts fastened it, but these had been unlocked. He opened the door, looked out on the side of the Land Office, the dark side of the hill stretching below to the city.

"That was Barney Vale got away, I reckon," he muttered.

He stepped outside, but saw none of his enemies. They had run for it, disappearing in the night.

"You there! Reach, and step out slow!"

The sharp command told him it was one of the Austin policemen, who had started around the building and had spied him as he stood near the door.

"All right Marshal!" he called. "Don't shoot. I'm Ranger Hatfield."

It was an officer he knew, a man named Tim Willis. When Willis recognized the tall Ranger, he swore in amazement.

"What in tarnation's goin' on up here, Hatfield? You savvy who the two young hombres up front are?"

"I can tell yuh all about it, Willis," the Ranger said quickly. "But first, let's hustle down to Barney Vale's office. Them killers might stop there. I'll give yuh the story on the way."

Willis hurried with him to meet the other officers who were on their way to the Land Office. En route to Vale's office, Hatfield informed the police that an attempt had been made to enter the file room.

Vale's office and the living quarters behind it were dark. The Ranger and the marshals went inside, guns ready, but the land shark and his men had not come back to their headquarters. A quick search was made through the town, but evidently Vale had taken alarm and fled the city.

Returning to the Land Office, they found that Five-Finger Henny, whom Hatfield had shot at the corner was stiff and cold. The Ranger would never mistake that member of Vale's gang — the Joker. But the joke was on Five-Finger now.

A city marshal was hovering over Keith Warden and Frank Garrett, who had been taken into the file room. Warden's wound was through the flesh of his upper arm just below the shoulder. It had been roughly dressed and the bleeding had almost stopped. A lamp had been lighted, and on one of the tables stood a pen and a bottle of ink which had been overturned. In the stacks, two paper-wrapped files lay on the floor where they had fallen.

"Any files missin', Garrett?" inquired the Ranger.

"I'll have to check up," Frank told him. Warden had informed Frank that the tall man was a friend, and Frank was aware anyway that Hatfield had saved his life that night.

Young Garrett checked through the files and, after a time, he nodded.

"There's two gone, at least," he said. "One takes in the land near Tate's, but I believe the other, accordin' to the missin' number, would be a lot farther west. Reagan County, mebbe."

"That's north of the Edwards Plateau, ain't it?"

"Yeah, reckon so."

Jake Jervis's Lazy J lay in Reagan, and Hatfield did not doubt but that Barney Vale, the land shark, had come to the Land Office that night to work on the supposed problem which Jervis had posed to Vale at Hatfield's suggestion. The Ranger was uneasy about the other file, though, which contained the records on the section of Gillespie County in which George Tate's ranch and other properties were inscribed.

Hatfield had overheard Vale tell Sam Ince, his aide in the land frauds, that he intended to clear out Tate, and with them the Garretts, who had found refuge with their relatives.

The amateur sleuthing of Frank Garrett and Keith Warden had wrecked Hatfield's careful plan to trap Barney Vale and catch him in the act of altering land records. Yet Hatfield could not be too harsh with the young fellows. They had been eager to snare the land shark and had strong personal reasons for doing it.

The Ranger spent the remainder of the night in Austin, for there was nothing more he could do before morning. The police had an alarm out for Vale and his gang, and a careful search was being made. . . .

In the morning, reporting to the keenly interested McDowell, who was chagrined at having missed the fight at the Land Office the night before, Hatfield said:

"Cap'n, I ain't shore where Vale's run to. He's on the prod, though, that's a cinch. He's got a couple of files and mebbe he's headed west, to work on them sections. He won't quit easy. I'll have to get on the rascal's trail."

"Go to it, Hatfield," said Captain Bill. "And don't fergit — if there's any way to do it, let me in on the arrest. I'll see to the warrants here, chargin' Vale with enterin' and tamperin' with files in the Land Office."

CHAPTER X
ON THE TRAIL

Before riding out of Austin, on Barney Vale's trail, Hatfield called on Jake Jervis of the Lazy J, his rancher friend who had given him a hand in his attempt to draw Vale out.

In reply to the Ranger's request, Jervis nodded.

"I can make Vanceville on my way home," he said. "It ain't but a few miles out of the way. I'll be pullin' out in a day or two — can hardly wait to see the twins again, the cute critters. But I'll stick with you as long as the Rangers need me, Hatfield."

"*Bueno.* I believe Vale stole the file with the land records of yore district, Jake. He's on the prod, for fair. Somethin's hurried him, and Garrett and Warden have panicked him. I'll either meet yuh or leave a message with the bartender at the Golden Horns in Vanceville, savvy? I may need yuh."

Keith Warden's arm was sore and stiff. It had to have attention, careful dressing, and

Warden was living up in Frank Garrett's room. Sue's brother had escaped with scratches and cuts in the desperate battle at the Land Office.

Admonishing them both to be careful, Hatfield rode out of town, westward. He meant to visit Vanceville, and Big Ed Pallette's E P, believing that Vale might head that way.

When he reached Vanceville, however, Barney Vale was not in the town. Discreet inquiry by the Ranger brought him the information that the man he sought had not been seen in Vanceville for days.

"He's mighty tough, and he savvies Warden and Garrett will talk," mused the Ranger, as he fingered his whisky glass in the Golden Horns late that afternoon. "He'll mebbe hide out for a while, at the Epe or some other place, till he's straightened things out to suit himself."

Pallette, the owner of the E P, was Vale's accomplice, whether the horse-faced rancher liked it or not, and Vale would do as he pleased on the ranch.

Hanging around the saloon, Hatfield had decided to step up the road and get supper at the Texas Lunch when he saw Big Ed Pallette ride up, drop his horse's reins over the rack in front of the Golden Horns, and duck under. There were four men — Hatfield recognized them as toughs he had seen when at the E P — tagging after Pallette, and they trailed the rancher inside the saloon. But Barney Vale was not with Pallette.

The cowman went to the bar. His long face was even longer than usual, and he looked miserable, broken in spirit. He hardly replied to the greetings of acquaintances in the saloon. He put down money, and the barkeeper pushed out a bottle and glass. Pallette began to drink, one shot after another, throwing them down fast, his booted foot on the rail as he hung over the counter. The four gunnies who had come in with him drifted down the bar, in a knot by themselves.

Hatfield sat down at a table in a corner and ordered a beer, when the waiter came up to him. He could see Pallette's face in the mirror, could see the dejected droop of the rancher's body.

"He ain't satisfied with his bargain, I reckon," decided the Ranger. "Vale's got him down."

He wondered if Big Ed, who had so gleefully hired Vale to shove out the Garretts and others, was aware that the great E P would fall into Vale's hands in case Pallette dropped dead by some quirk of Fate — such as a six-gun slug.

Pallette was ossifying himself as rapidly as possible, pouring in the burning red-eye to numb his sensations — or perhaps his conscience. He was obviously sorry for himself.

The four toughs who had come in with the E P owner drank with less abandon. After a while two of them went over to the Annex, picked out girls, and danced with them.

Hatfield hung around on the chance that Vale might show up, but the man did not come in. However, when Pallette had been there about an hour, the bat-wings slammed in, and Sheriff Al Craig appeared. The Golden Horns was filled with cowmen and their hands, townsmen, and gamblers. Music banged in the Annex across from the barroom. The floor shook as heavy boots pounded away in the dance.

The lean, weathered Craig stopped short as he saw Pallette. Hatfield saw the scowl on the sheriff's face. Craig's stringy, faded mustache bristled, the ends rising. The muscles in his leathery cheeks, one of which was bulged by his tobacco cud, went taut.

"Cuss yuh, Pallette!" sang out Craig. "Are you in on this dispossess of George Tate? A fat tarantula named Sam Ince come along, and he's got iron-clad papers showin' *he* owns Tate's ranch! What in tarnation blazes is goin' on? The whole country's gone loco!"

Craig was in a towering rage. He was evidently an honest soul, decided Hatfield, who was being forced to carry out unpleasant edicts of the law. The sheriff was in the position of putting old friends off their lands, driving them from their homes, and it sickened him.

At the sound of Craig's harsh voice, Big Ed Pallette slowly turned. His deep-set eyes were bleary, and he teetered, holding to the bar with one hand.

"Wash — what — huh? Oh, 'lo Al — drink up."

But Craig was too angry to maintain even a pretense of friendliness. He shook his head.

"I wouldn't drink with you, not if I was in the desert and dyin' for a snorter, savvy? For two cents and a rusty collar button I'd run yuh over to the calaboose and toss yuh in for disorderly conduct! Shut up!"

Pallette blinked. He would not rise to any challenge. He was broken. No doubt Big Ed had been largely instrumental in placing Al Craig in office, but an honest man could go just so far.

Craig snorted in disgust, stalked down the bar and slammed a silver dollar on the counter. He had a quick drink by himself, glaring around, but nobody caught his eye or said anything to upset him further.

"So," thought Hatfield, "Vale has Ince actin' as his front to take over George Tate's!"

Mrs. Garrett and Sue had taken refuge at their cousin's place, and now Vale was stealing Tate's ranch and sweeping across the county — and on into Kimble County, where Ince already had seized great stretches of Texas soil.

The quartet of so-called cowboys who had come in with big Ed Pallette carried the unconscious rancher out around midnight, tied him on his mustang, and returned to the E P. Hatfield trailed them out, along the moonlit dirt road from Vanceville to the ranch.

He left Goldy out from the Epe and sneaked in, looking for Barney Vale. But the land shark was not in the main house. The gunnies dumped Big Ed on the couch, blew out the lamp on the table, and went to turn in themselves.

Hatfield silently drew away. He was uneasy, with Barney Vale out of sight. There was no guessing what Vale might be up to next, except that it would be evil. The

Ranger was tired after many long hours in the saddle, and he slept in the chaparral, rolled in his blanket. . . .

Next day, from a hilltop, Hatfield watched Sheriff Al Craig as the officer rode alone to George Tate's spread. The Ranger saw the white legal document which Craig handed to George Tate. It was a preliminary notice, no doubt, that Tate must show cause why he was occupying land that did not belong to him. Unless Tate was able to prove his title, later steps would dispossess the rancher.

Tate would certainly have a deed. The deed would have been recorded at a certain time and date in the Austin land records. Yet unless these records upheld the claim, Tate would be in a hopeless position.

"Vale's fixed up Tate's file, like he done the others," concluded the Ranger.

He had spied on Craig only in order to start on Vale's trail. He was behind the sheriff when the lawman started back toward his Vanceville headquarters. Craig was halfway home, when a rider came from a clump of brush near the rough trail, accosting the sheriff. Craig stopped to talk for a moment. Hatfield recognized the man who had ridden up as Sam Ince, Barney Vale's stout aide. Craig spoke with Ince, then shook a fist in the fellow's face, and rode on.

Ince rode southwest. Hatfield dropped Craig, picked up Ince's trail. It led to another small settlement, a sleepy little cowtown called Springdale.

Springdale was not so lively as Vanceville, nor so big. Two main rows of buildings faced each other across a dusty plaza. There were three saloons, one of which took roomers. Ince paused at the bar of one of them, had a couple of drinks and came out. Vale's fat aide rode to a small frame house, its weathered boards lacking paint and black from the sun, where he went inside.

There were three or four armed men outside. Three were sitting on a board bench, and a fourth was leaning with his back to the rear wall. They looked like guards to the Ranger.

Hatfield kept out of sight, observing the building into which Sam Ince had disappeared. But nothing happened.

He hung around Springdale all afternoon. Siesta time found the settlement practically asleep. It was not until dark fell that Ince and Barney Vale emerged from the small frame house, mounted saddled horses which had been brought up, and rode away, with six gunnies behind them.

The Ranger hesitated. It might be hard to follow them in the night, and he had noted no baggage to indicate that Vale might be leaving his hideout permanently. A small lamp still burned in the little building, and the front door stood ajar.

"I reckon he'll be back, and this is as good a chance as any to look over his stuff," he decided.

He had seen to Goldy earlier, and hidden the sorrel in a stable near at hand. The saloons were open and doing a good business, for the night was warm.

Hatfield went around to the rear of the house from which Vale had emerged. A window was partly open, and he could look into the kitchen, see on through a hall into the front room. One of Vale's killers sat in a chair by the table, reading a newspaper by the lamplight.

After a while the man yawned, stretched, and dropped the paper. He rose, pacing restlessly back and forth. He went out on the stoop, returned. Music came from the biggest saloon and he looked in that direction. He had been left to watch the hideout, and he was bored. Besides he evidently believed that Vale had little fear of being discovered in Springdale, where he had run after the trouble in Austin.

The Ranger waited. If the guard did not soon turn in, or go out for a drink, Hatfield meant to strike him down. The man had a flask. He drained it, and closed and bolted the front door. Then he blew out the lamp. Hatfield heard the floor creaking under the guard's weight as Vale's man stretched out on a bunk along the wall.

It was not long until snores told the Ranger that the fellow was asleep. The back door was bolted, but the window was not. Softly he pushed it wide enough, and climbed through, crouching under it for a moment. He had the floor plan fairly well in mind as he kept near the wall, where the boards would not creak so much, and reached the front room.

He was within a few feet of the bunk when the sentry's snoring broke its rhythm. The big Ranger froze where he was, hand poised to whip out his Colt.

"Ugh — ugh! Say, that you, boss? Didn't take yuh long to fix Pallette's clock. What time is it, anyway?"

"Ev'rything's all right, pard," said the Ranger softly.

"What?"

Sleep had dulled the guard's senses. He had started awake, perhaps from the vibration as the big officer crossed the flimsy

123

flooring, and had jumped to the conclusion, as an awakening person often does, that he had been sleeping for a long time.

Hatfield loomed over him. His mind becoming fully alert, the killer muttered a curse and brought his legs around so he could leap from bed. Hatfield could see the man's body silhouetted against the lighted rectangle of the side window. He slashed at the man's head with his heavy Colt barrel, made a full connection on his second try. The killer had tried to reach his pistol in the holster hanging from the end of the bunk, but hadn't made it.

In the dim light, Hatfield checked the limp figure across the bunk. A gag, and bonds made from the blanket, secured the sentry.

The Ranger worked swiftly then. He had comprehended what the gunny had said about Big Ed Pallette. He was convinced that Vale and his gang had ridden to the E P, there to dispose of Pallette, whose usefulness to Vale was no doubt ended.

"I want Pallette," the Ranger thought grimly, but first he would take a few minutes to check up at Vale's hideout.

He located a candle stub, lighted it, kept it shaded by his hand. There was a leather bag on a shelf in the kitchen cupboard. It contained papers — the two missing files from the General Land Office at Austin and other interesting documents!

CHAPTER XI
PALLETTE'S DOOM

Hatfield, crouched by the iron cookstove in the corner which hid the candle and gave him some protection in case Vale or some of his men came back, studied the documents he had found.

There were deeds, in Vale's or Ince's names, or showing joint control such as Vale had arranged with Pallette and Larsen of the Triangle 3. The deeds were in perfect order, recorded and stamped.

"I reckon Vale's fixed the files they belong in and put 'em back," thought the Ranger. "Let's see — what's this map?"

It was a map which showed several central Texas counties, a large-scale reproduction of a section of the Lone Star State. A line had been drawn by a pen from Austin westward and bearing thence northwestward, to the city of San Angelo, an important center.

"Passes through E P range, through what

was Garrett's, and on Tate's ranch." The ranger nodded. "Then into Kimble — Porter's land and that of others. Why, it's all laid out!"

Barney Vale had control of long stretches of acreage bordering the tenuous line!

There were other papers which Hatfield looked over quickly, for further hints. In the back of his mind, as he studied Vale's secret records, was the urgency that he must somehow save Big Ed Pallette from death. Pallette might prove to be a valuable witness against Vale.

A sheet of notepaper had been crumpled up, then smoothed out, and saved as valuable by Barney Vale. It was a letter to the land shark, a hasty scrawl which read:

The matter concerning you will be brought up in the Legislature at next session — in about two weeks. Nothing can hold its public announcement off any longer.

Rice

"Rice," muttered the Ranger. "Wonder if that's the State Senator?"

He recalled having seen Vale receive a letter in the land agent's Austin office. Vale had seemed perturbed, had balled the paper in his hand, then retrieved it. Perhaps it was this warning from a secret connection in high quarters. And such a missive would have blackmail value, if nothing else, to such a dealer as Barney Vale.

"It should tie Vale up plenty if I take these papers," he thought. "Still, he's recorded as owner of a lot of land along that line."

He put the documents back in the brown leather bag and set it by the back window.

The gun guard in the front room was grunting. He was still dazed but coming back to life. Hatfield cut his bonds, removed the gag. Then he quickly left by the rear window, as he had come, carrying the bag with him.

Hurrying up the sidewalk, he paused at the big saloon. At the front of the bar stood a town marshal, surveying the scene. He wore a round badge on his gray shirt.

The tall Ranger stepped in, touched the marshal on the sleeve.

"Texas Ranger," he murmured. "Step outside, will yuh, Marshal?"

The town officer blinked, but obeyed with alacrity. On the stoop, the rays from the lighted windows sheened on the silver star circle, emblem of the mighty Rangers, held in Hatfield's cupped palm.

"Yessuh, Ranger, what can I do for yuh?"

asked the marshal.

"I'm in a powerful hurry. Can yuh round up a posse and foller me to the E P Ranch?"

"Do my best, Ranger. It's outside my jurisdiction, though. The county sheriff is Al Craig, at Vanceville."

"I savvy that. But this is a matter of life or death. Get what fighters yuh can and hurry to the E P. I'll go on ahead."

The marshal nodded and hurried back into the saloon, where he could pick out men for the posse. Hatfield went on to the corral next to the livery stable where he had left Goldy. A young fellow of about sixteen, the night wrangler, was on duty.

"You look like yuh can ride, son," said the tall Ranger. "I'll give yuh ten dollars if yu'll saddle yore best runner and make Vanceville tonight."

The lad was willing. He woke a Mexican wrangler who was asleep in another part of the stable. Taking the notes hastily scrawled by Hatfield, and the money, he went to saddle his horse.

The Ranger set out on the golden sorrel, hoping he would be in time to snatch Big Ed Pallette from Vale's deadly grip. . . .

It was an hour past midnight when Hatfield sighted the yellow lamp burning in the Epe ranchhouse. The bunkhouse and other buildings were dark in the pale moonshine.

His saddle-bags, in which he usually carried iron rations, a spare shirt and other necessities during his long excursions in the name of Texas law, bulged with papers. The satchel had proved a bulky nuisance, flapping against Goldy's ribs and annoying the sorrel.

So the Ranger had stuffed the documents into the leather pockets and tossed away Vale's grip, for he needed to make time. From what the sentry at Vale's Springdale hideout had said, Hatfield was convinced the land shark meant to kill Big Ed Pallette.

Vale's game was becoming clearer and clearer, as the sinister land agent clamped his talons on Texas. It was a big game, the stakes running into millions, should Vale win. And only Hatfield could check the man.

Hatfield drew in as close to the ranchhouse as he dared on horseback, and dismounted.

"Wait, Goldy," he whispered, stroking the arched, warm neck of the beautiful sorrel. "I'll call when I need yuh."

He did not need to drop the reins for the sorrel would wait patiently in the vicinity until Hatfield whistled for him. The Ranger had trained the gelding for such a situation.

Hatfield made ready, hanging his heavy spurred boots on the saddle-horn, substituting supple moccasins which he carried for such excursions as that upon which he was embarked tonight. He rubbed dirt on his face and hands to kill the sheen of the skin, left his Stetson, tying his black locks back out of his eyes with his bandanna. He carried his two Colts, and ammunition, in his pockets.

Hatfield flitted toward the house. The spread lay peacefully in the night. It took a little time to creep close, using bits of concealment such as a low bush, a jutting rock, the contours of the uneven, grass-studded yard.

Pressed flat to the warm, sandy dirt, the Ranger could hear the low hum of men's voices. A cigar end glowed ruby red on the porch, as someone passed through the lighted doorway. On the other side of the house stood a number of saddled mustangs, stamping the ground, whinnying low now and then.

During Hatfield's first investigations, he had learned something of Big Ed Pallette. The rancher was a widower. He had a couple of daughters but they were grown up, married, and lived elsewhere. Save for his hired help, the horse-faced Texan lived alone, alone with the overweening ambition which had forced him to throw in his lot with Barney Vale.

Greedy for more and more land, for power, Pallette had agreed to Vale's schemes, no doubt believing that all he had to do was to pay off Vale when the land shark had disposed of their victims. Unaware of Vale's master plan, or that the E P was but a part of it, Pallette was riding straight toward death. Vale had meant all along to use Pallette and dispose of him finally when the proper time came.

That moment seemed to have arrived, mused Hatfield. The Ranger wasted no sympathy on Pallette, however, for the man had become a willing tool of Vale's. He did desire to keep the E P owner alive. Pallette could ruin Vale in a court of law. Vale was clever, slippery, and strong witnesses would be needed to convict him.

Pallette might already have been killed. There would have been no one to interfere, because decent cowboys, such as Keith Warden, who had ridden for the Epe, had quit in disgust or been discharged at Vale's order. Now hired guns controlled by the land shark had been taken on. They were paid by Pallette, but Vale gave them their orders.

The Ranger started, cocked his ear. Through the night, a singer was approaching the E P, on the road from Vanceville. The men on the porch heard the rider coming, and some of them mounted and rode to meet him.

From the vantage point Hatfield had reached, he sighted Barney Vale, slouched in the open doorway of the house. Then he saw that rider who sang as he rode was Big Ed coming home, after an evening of wassail in town. Three or four of Vale's killers were with him. They never let him out alone, it appeared. Now others joined the procession, grinning at the big rancher's bellowings. The words grew distinguishable as Pallette came up the lane, riding a big white gelding with a gray mane:

Oh, she promised to meet me when the
    clock struck seventeen,
At the stockyards ten miles out of town.
Where the cows and the heifers and the
    old fat Texas steers,
Sell for beefsteak at ten counts a pound!
She's my darlin', my daisy, she's hump-
    backed, she's lazy,

She's cross-eyed, bowlegged and lame,
And they say her teeth are false —

Pallette came closer in the circle of light
from the door. He slid off his horse, fell to
his hands and knees, crawled a few feet
toward the steps. A couple of grinning
outlaws seized his arms and hoisted him up,
supporting him and running him up the
stairs, where Barney Vale coldly stared at
the lax face.

"You pig, Pallette," said Vale contemptu-
ously. "You drunken fool!"

"Wash wrong, pard? Wash wrong?"

They shoved Pallette through the door
and the impetus carried him in. He fell flat
on his face on the carpet.

Everybody wanted to see the sport. A
drunk was always a source of amusement to
such fellows, and Vale's killers bunched in
the front of the main room to watch.

"Get up!" ordered Vale.

Hatfield crawled closer, up under one of
the open windows halfway down the side of
the long wing. He could see the big comfortable living room, with the jutting fireplace
built of cemented round stones, to his left.
Toward the wall, the fireplace bulge made a
small alcove, open only to the room in front.

Amused toughs raised Pallette, who was

sodden with drink. He had no doubt been senseless, but the fresh air and the jogging had brought him partially back to consciousness. As the gun guards pushed him into an armchair, the rancher shook his head.

"Give me a drink," he muttered.

At Vale's nod, someone poured one from the flask on the table. In Pallette's condition, it could only help revive him.

Vale folded his arms. His stout form was clad in black pants and a white shirt. His chestnut hair was combed sleek, but could not conceal the bald spot. His fierce violet eyes glinted as he whipped himself into killing rage against his erstwhile accomplice.

"I've stood all I'm going to from you, Pallette!" he snarled. "You've made a jackass out of yourself and I'm through with you. The boys say you can't hold your liquor. You shoot off your mouth like a kid when you have a few. You've made threats against me. You've talked too much!"

"R-rowr!"

Pallette shook his head, clearing his throat. He hardly heard what was said. He tried to focus his flickering eyes on Vale.

Vale stepped close, slapped him across the mouth. Pallette straightened up, while a hurt expression came over his long face. He

135

put both hands on the chair arms, as though to rise.

"Washa idee? Who hit me?"

A half-circle of sadistic killers crowded between Hatfield and the nauseating scene as Vale and his men made ready to kill Pallette.

There was one lamp on the center table. Pallette was centered in its light, helpless, an easy target.

"You're goin' to get what's coming to you, Pallette," said Vale. "You're going to die!"

CHAPTER XII
THE FIGHT AT THE
E P

Somehow Big Ed comprehended. Perhaps the ominous tone, or the deadly attitude of Vale pierced the liquor fog in his brain. His eyes widened as he realized that death was at hand.

"Vale — don't!" he mumbled.

The shock had somewhat sobered him, but his whole body trembled as though with palsy. His calloused hands gripped at the chair arms. Once again he started up.

"Look out, he's pullin' his gun, boss!" shouted a killer, in mock alarm.

They were at the point of finishing Pallette and Hatfield had to shoot, for Barney Vale had shifted, reaching for a hidden pistol in his pocket. The bullet hastily sent by the Ranger, as he bobbed up at the open window, slashed the arm of a gunman, tore through and struck Vale, who went down among his gang.

The Ranger's second bullet — a flash

behind the first, ripped into the bunched killers, while the startling explosions filled the room.

"Watch it!" shrieked a Vale henchman.

The hired killers were scattering, their attention diverted to the window through which the gunfire had come. Guns were flying into outlaw hands. Pallette was on his feet. He staggered off toward the rear of the house where he fell to the mat. Bullets whined over his head.

Hatfield saw Vale's men dashing out of the lighted room, making for the open front door, their bullets, hurriedly shot, singing his way. He had to put out the light. His third slug smashed the lamp chimney, instantly extinguishing the flame.

"Pallette — this way!" he called sharply.

He wanted to get the rancher outside, if possible. A groan answered him. Wounded foes were swearing, begging for help. Hatfield wondered if Vale had been hit, and if so, how badly.

The confusion would not last long. Hatfield ducked down, ran to the next window toward the rear, and dived through it into the room.

Keeping low, as the outlaw bunch blasted at the opening from which he had shot, the Ranger groped with his left hand for Pallette. He heard the rancher grunting, cursing, not far from where the man had fallen.

"I'm a friend, Pallette! Quick! come along!"

"I — I can't use my leg!" gasped the cowman. "Bullet!" Fear and shock had sobered Pallette.

The Vale men were calling to one another, and some had started around the house. Hatfield had hoped to pick up Pallette and escape by the back way, but Big Ed was down, so that could not be done.

"There they are, over in the corner!" howled somebody, and a Colt flamed, the lead ploughing the floor close to the Ranger and Pallette.

"Roll, cuss it!" snapped Hatfield.

Pallette obeyed. Hatfield seized his shoulder, shoved him into the niche formed by the bulge in the facing of the stone fireplace. With the walls, it gave protection from three sides.

The moments lost by Pallette proved fatal to Hatfield's bold plan, though. He turned, meaning to rush out the rear door, whistle up Goldy, and make his own escape, for Pallette hardly deserved to have anyone sacrifice life for him. But he heard more men coming through the kitchen. They were Vale hirelings who had been asleep in the bunkhouse.

Hatfield kicked over a long, thick-topped table which had been standing along the wall. With a couple of chairs, it formed a rough barricade toward the open room.

"Draw yore gun, Pallette, and fight for yore life!" he commanded, crouched by the moaning rancher.

Cool in peril, icy nerves of steel enjoying the danger, Ranger Hatfield made his stand.

Pallette pulled himself together. He had a pistol, and he drew it, cocked it.

"Who are you, mister?" he demanded. "Vale — they were goin' to drill me!"

"Name's Hatfield — tell yuh more later. Right now, we got to defend ourselves. Watch yore side, and keep behind the table."

"Vale's got thirty men, anyways," growled Pallette.

"Keep yore dander up. There's help comin'."

Their snarling guns had told Vale's gang they were still fighting. But also, their position was known. There was a lull, as the gunnies took stock. Hatfield crouched at the right side of the barricade, Colt up, hammer spur back under his thumb. He strained his ears, trying to hear what was being said. The Vale men were talking together and he could catch sounds of them from every side.

Every minute was a gain for the Ranger. He had been at the E P for over an hour, and it was now after two o'clock, so the posse from Springdale must be well on the way.

Pallette kept grunting. His leg, sliced by a chunk of metal, ached and bled.

Somebody bobbed up at the nearest window, a few feet from the barricade, fired rapidly, the flaming powder seeming to light the whole room. Hatfield sent a slug into the opening. The pistol there suddenly stopped, and there was a dull thud under the window. Other guns, across the way, blasted into the table and wall, ripping splinters from the wood, smashing the adobe to plaster.

There was another lull. Hatfield reloaded the Colt he had been using, placed it on the floor close at hand. He drew his spare, kept it up and ready.

"Pallette! You in there?"

The hail came from the window but nobody was framed in the rectangle lighted by the moonlight. It was Barney Vale's voice. The land shark who lay under the window was calling to the rancher.

"Answer him," whispered Hatfield, thinking that Vale couldn't be too badly hit, if he could move around and talk.

"What yuh want, Vale?" growled Pallette.

"Who's that with you?" demanded Vale. "You're actin' like a dumb fool, Ed. We were only fooling. We never meant to kill you."

Pallette's strangled laugh told Vale that he was not that much of a dumb fool, that Vale's argument was absurd.

"You'd better come out," Vale called. "I give you my word you won't be hurt if you surrender. Toss out your guns and walk along with your hands up. We'll let you go."

"Oh, yeah?" said Pallette, his voice dripping sarcasm. "Yuh dirty cuss, Vale, yuh wrecked me! I'd rather die here with a gun in my hand than give up. So'd my pard."

"Who is he? I'm sure he's not Craig."

"Don't yuh wish yuh knowed?" taunted Pallette.

Vale gave up his attempt to parley, to trick the two into coming out. He withdrew. After a time, they caught, with hypersensitive ears, noises on the front porch. Their eyes accustomed to the darkness now, they could make out the lighter windows and the doorway.

To their left, around the heavy stone facing of the hearth, lay two or three of Vale's men from whom occasionally they heard a whisper or the creak of a leather belt.

Otherwise, the big room was clear. Vale's paid killers would not venture inside, for Ranger guns had cut them.

A heavy explosion whooshed from the front window directly in line with the niche. A bullet hit the table, split it, moved it with its force.

"Buffalo gun!" gasped Hatfield, stunned by the closeness of it. Two or three more would wreck the barricade!

Flat on his stomach, he edged to the side of the table, thrust his Colt past it. He watched for a faint outline, for the gunner must raise to fire with any aim. In a moment he saw the sheen of moonlight on a long rifle barrel, the head and shoulder of the marksman. He fired twice, and the buffalo gun clattered inside the room.

"What's that?" grunted Pallette, as new sounds reached his ears.

Shouts, the thudding of galloping horses, came from the west side of the ranch. Guns opened up, and Hatfield felt relief, was sure that the marshal from Springdale had arrived with his posse. Turned from the penned men in the house, the Vale killers were battling against the new threat.

"Look out, feller, them lobos are still lyin' just around the fireplace," warned Pallette, as Hatfield started out.

A slug fired hastily told the Ranger that Pallette was right.

Outside, blasting gun fire and the loud cries of fighting men rang out in the night. For a time it was close in. It began to recede, and died off to scattered shots, then to silence.

Soon they heard galloping horses coming back. There was a pale touch of gray in the eastern sky. In half an hour, the sun of a new day would bathe the world in its beauty.

"Yuh reckon that was the help yuh expected?" said Pallette, with a gulp.

"Reckon so," muttered Hatfield. "That Springdale marshal didn't fetch along enough men."

There was a flareup of noise not far from the house, on the side from which Hatfield had come. He heard men yelling.

"Run him thisaway!" someone howled. "I'll rope him!"

Heavy hoofs beat the earth and a horse screamed.

Hatfield swore. "Sounded like Goldy! They must have sighted him when they chased off that posse!"

A bullet came within an inch of his face and he drew back. The men were still waiting, just around the bulge of the hearth.

A couple of carbines snapped outside, and

then quiet once more reigned.

Hatfield felt the deepest anxiety, over Goldy's fate. The sorrel would not allow others to catch him, but in driving after the posse, they must have flushed Goldy from the bushes. They had tried to rope him, then fired at the magnificent animal.

"Recognized him, I s'pose," he thought, biting his lip hard. He could hardly bear the thought of losing the gelding.

"Dawn's come," announced Big Ed Pallette.

The world had imperceptibly grown visible. Even inside, they could see the shapes of chairs, and the body of a Vale gunslinger near the door. The room was wrecked — chairs and tables overturned, the rug kicked up, fresh bullet scars in walls and floor.

"I smell smoke!" cried Pallette suddenly.

Hatfield had already sniffed the telltale odor of burning wood. The dawn had brought a rising fresh southwest breeze. On the windward side, Vale had ordered a wood fire built and it was eating at the window frame. There was a yellow flare there.

"Kerosene!" said Hatfield. "They just tossed a jug of it into the room!"

The oil carried the flames, which quickly took hold of inflammable materials inside. Acrid smoke caught at nostrils and eyes.

The outlaws who had been waiting around the fireplace, had slipped away.

"It won't be long," said Pallette dismally.

He could see his companion now, the tall man who had saved him. There was awe and fear in Pallette's red-shot eyes. His face was chalky, and his trouser leg a mess of bloody cloth. Even with the dirt staining the Ranger's face, the rancher thought he recognized him.

"Say, ain't you the hombre who rode up and asked me for a job?"

"That's right," the Ranger answered.

"Who are yuh, anyways? All I know is yuh done yore best to save my neck."

"I'll tell yuh when we get to Hades," Hatfield said grimly.

They seemed near that place, with the rising heat and flames, the choking, acrid smoke which made eyes water and made them start coughing.

"They'll shoot us down when we run out," growled Pallette.

"That's their idea," Hatfield said, in a monotone.

The fire had a voice, an increasingly loud roar. But the fireplace stone protected them from it to an extent, and nearby was the open north window. But the fire had a breath which licked at them, reflected from the ceiling and walls. The floor was getting hot.

"We — we got to have air!" gasped Hatfield. "Let's go, Pallette!"

He helped Big Ed crawl to the end of the table.

"Make the winder and fall out and come up shootin'!" ordered the officer. "I'll cover yuh as well as I can."

Pallette pulled himself up, holding with his left hand, weight on his right leg. Hatfield, blinded by smoke, singed by the hot air blowing through the room, staggered after the rancher, facing death from waiting enemy guns.

Chapter XIII
Escape

Grit, and the instinct which drives man from fire saved the Ranger, for the smoke had nearly overcome him. Pallette lay over the sill, head hanging out. Hatfield somehow shoved him all the way over and, with retching coughs, tumbled from the opening on top of the prostrate rancher.

The draught sucked a thick gray vapor from the burning room. Though the walls were made of adobe brick, there was plenty of tinder-dry trim, and the roof was of wooden shingle slabs. The voice of the fire was terrifying, an increasing roar which aroused the primitive dread of men and animals near it.

Under the whitewashed wall away from the main blaze, Hatfield fought for clarity of mind, for the strength to raise a Colt and make a last fight. The clouds of smoke half-hid the huddled figures of Big Ed and the officer. Close to the ground, protected for the time being from the heat, there was fresh air, wonderful air that the lungs would accept without retching or heaving.

The tall Ranger's ears were roaring, pounding. He was confused, and it was difficult to distinguish whether that noise was in his own tortured brain or some outside source such as the conflagration.

Day had come. It was quite light although the sun had not yet risen. But in the small world occupied then by Hatfield, under the wall, dimness reigned. The few square feet were filled with acrid vapors, and the Ranger's burning eyes watered so he could not see.

Cracklings, a heavy thudding, a new rising note of threat from the fire told that a hole had been burned through the roof, allowing the fire to mushroom into the air. A ruby glow suffused all.

"Come on, Pallette, move!" gasped Hatfield.

The rancher lay crumpled as he had fallen; senseless. Hatfield crawled a foot and, with great effort, dragged Pallette after him. He rested, went on, his progress slow and painful. The breath of the fire seemed to pursue them.

But the air was better, and he was able to see objects. Teeth gritted, Colt in hand, the big officer watched for the enemy, sure they must be waiting for Pallette and himself to stagger from the smoke. He wanted to go down with a gun in his hand, fighting.

He had made fifty or sixty feet away from the burning building, but it was at great cost to his racked frame. He pulled Big Ed Pallette along as he might a limp, dead animal.

In top physical condition, trained to hardships, Hatfield began to gain a hold on himself, as his lungs recovered and his vision cleared. The roaring in his ears diminished. He could hear the voice of the fire behind him, but the confusion was leaving him.

He squatted on his haunches beside Pallette, still gasping. It was astounding that bullets did not tear into them, kill them. Vale had lit the fire to drive them out, but now that they were out, no gunfire came their way.

He began to make out other sounds than the immediate ones which had dominated his tiny orbit.

"Gunshots!" he muttered.

He thought the cracking firearms were to the north, perhaps northwest, of the E P buildings.

Water! It was a frantic thought. His lips

and throat were burning dry, he craved it in every pore. Since the first shock had passed, and he was out of immediate danger of death from the fire, he wanted a drink.

He left Pallette lying there and pushed himself up. He could stagger a few steps, and though his head felt light and his legs numb, he held himself up by sheer will. There was a springhouse through which water ran and he made it there. He plunged his face into the cool water, drank, and washed off some of the grime.

There was a tin dipper on a flat stone. He filled it and carried it back to Pallette. He gave the rancher several sips, and dashed the balance into his face. Pallette groaned, twitched.

"Reach, there!"

The command came from behind the Ranger, as he tended Pallette.

Slowly he glanced around. A horseman sat on a black mustang, regarding him, and also staring at him was the muzzle of a sawed-off shotgun.

"Sheriff Craig!" cried Hatfield.

"Drop that gun!" said the sheriff sternly.

Hatfield nodded, let go of his Colt. Craig whistled, and a couple of his possemen appeared.

"Check him," snapped Craig.

They came from the rear, felt for hidden weapons. They lifted Hatfield's spare Colt and his knife, then they brought out the silver star on silver circle, emblem of the Texas Rangers.

Al Craig swore hotly, jumping from his saddle.

"Yuh're Ranger Hatfield, huh? I got yore note the kid fetched from Springdale. Come as fast as we could. And Jake Jervis of the Lazy J told me yuh was all right."

"Yuh're in the nick, Sheriff," croaked Hatfield. "Vale and his bunch set fire to the house to drive us out on their guns."

He realized now what had occurred. The combined might of the two posses, as well as Jervis and his waddies, had forced Barney Vale to flee.

"Give the Ranger back his guns," ordered Craig. "Here's yore star, Hatfield."

The Ranger pinned the silver star on silver circle to his shirt front.

"Jervis and some of the young 'uns are tryin' to catch up with Vale," explained Craig. "But they had scouts out, and Vale had quite a start. A handful drawed us off north, too. I reckon the main party, with Vale, took off another way. There's three dead men lyin' around the ranch."

"It was quite a fight, Sheriff." Hatfield

squatted on his hunkers. His tobacco was ruined, and Craig handed him the "makin's." "I just had a plenty of smoke," drawled the Ranger, "but a quirly'll taste mighty fine."

Big Ed Pallette was coming to. Craig was looking over the rancher.

"Say, his leg's cracked, shore enough! Slug must have busted his prop."

When the sheriff fooled with the blood-soaked boot and pants leg, Pallette screamed in agony.

"Tie a rifle to it, get a blanket and make a stretcher," advised the Ranger. "Put him in the bunkhouse. When he can be moved to town, yuh'll hold him in jail, Sheriff. He's been in cahoots with Barney Vale, and he'll make a valuable witness."

"Yuh mean that?" Craig swore in delighted relief. "So yuh're over here after that lobo land shark! It made me sick at my stumick, the way him and Pallette treated the pore folks they ousted. I had to serve the papers, cuss it!"

"I savvy. Well, Vale's gone too far. The Rangers want him for killin's now."

Hatfield felt much better. He was washed out from what he had undergone but, unlike Pallette, he had no serious wound to cripple him, and his magnificent physical condition quickly asserted itself. He got up, whistled shrilly, to call Goldy, for he was worried over his horse.

The sorrel did not immediately answer, and Hatfield's anxiety grew.

"If Vale and his men shot him," he thought, "I'll take their hides off and hang 'em up to dry!"

But after a time he heard trotting hoofs, and a golden horse shape appeared, coming toward the men. They were still not far from the house, but had moved out of line of the smoke, which was heavy, since the entire center of the house was a mass of flames.

"That yore hoss?" inquired Craig, as he saw the Ranger put an arm over Goldy's withers while the gelding nuzzled him. "Nasty scrape he's got on his ribs."

The saddle, and Hatfield's other equipment — boots, Stetson and cartridge belt, as well as the papers he had taken from Vale's Springdale hideout, were all missing. Along Goldy's left side were abrasions with dirt ground into them. As he felt his horse over, Hatfield found a shallow groove close to Goldy's tail, where blood had oozed and clotted.

He remembered the scream he had heard, while he had been caught in the house by

Vale's men. He tried to figure what had occurred.

"Wish yuh could tell me, Goldy," he murmured. "Looks like when they couldn't rope yuh, they tried to crease yuh and stun yuh."

"I saw a saddle with busted cinches lyin' about a hundred yards off from the house, Ranger," volunteered a posseman.

"Take me to it," ordered Hatfield.

Craig insisted the Ranger borrow a horse, and he followed Craig's aide to the spot in the drifting smoke where the saddle lay. It was Hatfield's. The cinches had snapped, evidently when the sorrel had fallen from the violent shock of the wound. Boots, hat, and cartridge belt lay near at hand, but the saddle-bags were farther off. It was twenty minutes before he found them, tossed into a bush from which they were hanging.

The documents which Vale prized so highly, and which Hatfield had taken from the Springdale hideout, were, of course, missing.

The posse made a field headquarters in the E P bunkhouse, upwind from the ruined house. The fire was gutting Pallette's home. Big Ed had been carried to a bunk, and his wound washed and dressed as well as could be done in the emergency.

"Yuh can carry him to Vanceville in a wagon," advised Hatfield. "There's a sawbones there, ain't there?"

"Yep," Craig replied. "I'm mighty glad yuh come, Ranger. I got so's I hated that Vale's insides and I was thinkin' of quittin' this job. What was his game?"

"He's been grabbin' a stretch of land across Texas from Austin to San Angelo, Sheriff. He's an expert on titles and so forth, and he figgered out a scheme he thought was foolproof. Looked all legal-like to him."

"Where yuh s'pose the sidewinder'll head to?"

"I'd have said Springdale, before I found my saddle-bags," replied Hatfield. "But now I believe Vale'll run back to Austin. He's got a couple stolen files that need to be returned, in order to clinch his titles."

Barney Vale was still dangerous for he had the documents needed to prove his claims to the lands he had pirated: The Ranger, with Pallette's testimony, might be the only way to check the man.

Hatfield led Goldy to the watering trough, cleansed the sorrel's injuries, and turned him into a grassy corral. Then he joined Sheriff Craig who had broken open a padlocked shed to get food. They found a barrel of whisky, too, which they tapped.

After Hatfield had eaten, sleep nearly overcame him. His eyes were swollen, inflamed from smoke and lack of rest.

"I'll have to turn in for a while, Sheriff," he said.

"Go to it."

There were plenty of bunks. It was heavenly to drift off, after the strain of what he had undergone. . . .

The sun was bright and hot, nearly overhead, when Jim Hatfield came awake, refreshed, and hungry again. He got up. Pallette was lying on his bunk. The rancher looked ill. His face was pale and drawn, but his eyes were open, and he was watching the tall officer.

"So yuh're a Ranger!" he said. "I s'pose you're goin' to hold me."

"That's right, Pallette. Yuh shouldn't have played with Barney Vale."

"I'll take my medicine, Ranger. I've been a hog and a fool, but I'll try to make up to them folks."

Pallette was subdued, repentant. His attitude had been completely changed in the crucible of suffering.

A big golden cheese stood on the plank table, with liquor, crackers, and other edibles.

Hatfield carried over a drink and a handful of crackers and cheese to the rancher. The Ranger pulled up a bench, and the two men ate together.

"I'm glad yuh've come to yore senses, Pallette," Hatfield said. "Vale's a nasty customer. Yuh savvy he used yuh, to gain what he wanted, then he meant to finish yuh off when he was ready. Yore lands were held by you and him in joint control, so if you died, they went to Vale."

"I see," growled Pallette. "He crossed me, shore enough."

Since Vale had nearly killed him the night before, Pallette was ready to believe whatever evil might be told him of the land shark.

"You ain't the only rancher he tricked into actin' as a catspaw, either," Hatfield went on. "He used a string of big fellers like you to crush the small holders. How much did he charge yuh?"

"Plenty!" howled Pallette. "Hundred a week, just for his services, as he called it. He made me fire my best men and take on a passel of sidewinders and pay 'em! I couldn't get any work outa 'em, and the ranch was goin' to wrack and ruin."

"Yeah," said Hatfield, "you and Larsen and others paid Vale and his killer outlaws, while they planned to gun yuh all out."

Pallette was boiling against Vale.

"I saw Vale kill Lew Garrett, Ranger, and I'll swear to it! I never shot anybody myself, but Vale killed Possum Ransom and Garrett, and I believe he killed others. I'll take whatever's comin' to me, but I hope to live to see Vale stretch rope."

"Yuh will if he don't die of lead pizen first," promised Hatfield. "Yuh'll testify for the law, against Vale, I take it?"

"With pleasure!" cried Pallette.

"I'll do what I can for you, then, Pallette," said Hatfield. "Yuh got a Ranger's word for that."

Chapter XIV
An Old Man's Gun

As Hatfield and Pallette were finishing their meal, someone looked in through the bunkhouse door. It was Jake Jervis.

"Hatfield!" exclaimed the rancher. "Yuh're awake, huh? Mighty glad to see yuh."

The Pecos rancher came to shake his hand and grin at the big officer.

"I got yore note," Jervis said. "I'd hit Vanceville that evenin' with the boys on the way home. We hustled over with Craig. Just got back from chasin' Vale and his men, but our hosses was done in from the gallop we made out of town, and Vale had too much of a start for us."

"Jim!"

Hatfield turned, to see Keith Warden smiling, hurrying to greet him. Warden's left arm hung stiffly at his side, but he was in good condition save for the flesh wound in his shoulder.

"I was in Vanceville," he said quickly, "and

joined up with Craig and Jervis. I'm shore happy yuh're all right."

They talked over the big fight, and about how Vale had escaped into wild country below the Epe. Many of his followers had gone with him, and Vale had more killers throughout the long stretch of Texas land he had seized.

Hatfield did not wish to ride Goldy until the sorrel had had plenty of time to rest, after his injuries, but went to look after the mount. Jervis went back to help Craig and his possemen who were throwing buckets of water on the hot embers of the house. Pallette's home had been gutted, the adobe walls black, standing stark in the brilliant sunshine.

In the afternoon, a wagon was hitched up to a team and Pallette was carried to it to lie in its bed on folded blankets. Hatfield saddled an E P mustang, and led Goldy on a halter behind him. The fire was out, save for smoking ruins, as they started for Vanceville.

When they arrived in town, Big Ed Pallette was locked in the calaboose, at the southeast corner of the plaza. The town doctor was sent for to set the rancher's broken leg.

The prisoner was under the supervision of Sheriff Al Craig, while Keith Warden and other young men, sworn in as deputies, would help to guard him. Pallette showed no desire to escape, though. He was contrite, desiring only to make amends.

It was warm inside the adobe building, which was a wing of the city hall, and the three cells of the block were separated from Craig's office by a thick iron grille. But the men in the office could hear the physician working over Pallette, and the cowman's grunts of pain.

Hatfield sat on the edge of Craig's flat desk, while the sheriff, Warden and Jake Jervis gathered about him. Other men stood in the shade outside, talking over the fight at the E P, smoking, passing around flasks.

"What yuh reckon'll be Vale's next jump, Ranger?" asked Craig, filling his old briar pipe for a smoke.

"I'm convinced he'll head for Austin and try to return them stolen files to the Land Office," Hatfield said. "He'll have two main ideas — to put the records back so's they'll prove his claim, and to kill anybody who may wreck his game. Such as Pallette."

"Huh!" grunted the sheriff, frowning. "Yuh mean yuh believe Vale might try to grab Pallette out of here?"

"I do. He'd like to be rid of Pallette, and others as well — Keith Warden here, for one. Vale ain't beat yet, by a long shot. Where's the nearest telegraph?"

"There's a wire connection at Frederick," said Craig. "That's a good three hours from here by fast hoss."

"I'd like a trusty man to take a message there for me, and have it telegraphed to Austin headquarters," said the Ranger. "Got a pencil?"

Craig supplied him with writing materials, and Hatfield wrote off his warning to Captain McDowell. It read:

Set secret watch at Land Office. Believe Vale will attempt return of missing files. Will report soon as possible.

"Yuh're goin' to Austin again, then?" inquired the sheriff.

The Ranger nodded.

"I'm so shore Vale'll want to check up there, that I got to. Meanwhile, you boys stick here and keep close guard. Vale may send a bunch of gunhands to deal with Pallette. Be on the watch, and don't budge unless yuh hear from me otherwise. Savvy? I'll come myself or send a written order."

"I got yore note from Springdale, that the kid fetched, Ranger," Craig said. He felt in a shirt pocket, with surety the paper would be there, then tried others, a mystified look coming over his seamed, honest face. "Thought I had it in my clothes, but mebbe I stuck her in the drawer."

But a search proved that the note was not in the office.

"I could've dropped it, when I hurried out," the lawman said. "I was snoozin' on the couch here when the boy woke me."

"Never mind. I'll have to be movin' . . . Jervis, yuh can do me a real favor. I don't fancy the gait of that E P mustang I borrered. Can yuh loan me a good mount?"

"Yuh'll take my black, Star," answered Jake Jervis. "He's fast and smart, and a real hoss."

"Thanks, Jake. I want to give my sorrel a chance to let his wounds heal."

The Lazy J owner's best mount was a long-legged black gelding, with a white star on his forehead. He was mettlesome, a dancer. As the Ranger settled in the saddle, Star pranced about, but soon calmed down under the expert's soothing voice and hand.

"He's a honey, Jake," said Hatfield. "I'm obliged. I'll take good care of him. Be in touch soon as I can, gents. Keep a guard on Pallette day and night. I don't doubt Vale has spies here as well as in other places."

Hatfield set out on the run to the capital,

where McDowell would soon receive his warning about Barney Vale. It might prove a golden opportunity to trap the land shark, when he sought to replace the stolen land records. And Vale sparked the gigantic conspiracy which the Ranger's keen sleuthing had exposed. . . .

McDowell was waiting for his tall Ranger, when Hatfield rode the beautiful black gelding up to headquarters, dismounted, and started in. Hatfield had timed his entry into the city after dark, for he was aware that Vale might have agents watching Ranger movements. There was a good chance that Vale had discovered or guessed the identity of the tall man on the golden sorrel who had fought him so skillfully.

"Thought yuh'd be in, Jim," said McDowell, slapping Hatfield on the back. "I got dinner settin' for yuh. Knowed you'd be starved."

The old captain led him to the office where he had a snack and a bottle waiting. While Hatfield ate, McDowell gave him the news.

"Ain't seen hide nor hair of Vale. His office has been deserted since the fight at the Land Office that night. I got two trained men hid on the hill, and half a dozen armed recruits in the barracks ready to go into action at an instant's notice."

"I'll sashay over there and keep guard myself later," said Hatfield. "I got a hunch it'll be tonight, Cap'n. Vale wasn't too far ahead of me."

In fact, Vale could have reached town that morning, perhaps, had he come straight to Austin from the E P. But knowing he was wanted, the land agent would hardly show himself on the streets during daylight.

McDowell rose when Hatfield did. The old captain took his gun-belt from the peg on the wall, and buckled it on. He drew his Frontier Model Colt, checked the action, and made certain it was loaded and that the holster was supple and would not catch when the weapon was quickly drawn.

"I'm goin' along," he announced. "It ain't often I get a chance to have a little fun close to home."

Hatfield's gray-green eyes twinkled. He knew how McDowell felt. In his younger days, McDowell had been the best, a fast, hard fighter, as good as any man.

The two rode a roundabout way which brought them near to the General Land Office, looming on its steep hill. They dismounted and, in the shadows, began climbing. They would get in touch with the captain's Ranger agents who were up above.

There was a man at the rear of the building. He challenged in a whisper, and McDowell quickly replied.

"Nothin' yet, suh," reported the sentinel. "When I heard you, thought it might be somethin'."

They made themselves comfortable. Hatfield sat close to a small niche in the stone wall, from which point he could see the little side door which Vale had previously used.

It was a weary wait; hours passed. McDowell stuck with the Ranger, and the two guards were at their posts.

It was after midnight when the sentry who had been watching the rear of the massive building crept up to report.

"Cap'n! Somebody's comin' up the hill."

"All right. Keep it quiet, now. We'll watch till they come closer."

The Rangers strained their ears, peering into the blackness of the shadows. Sounds came, but many were from the city below, and in such dim light, stationary objects such as whitish stone or a clump of hedge, seemed to move.

McDowell touched Hatfield's arm. The old man's eyes were still sharp, and he had seen vague figures, two men, then several more, materialize from the darkness. They were making for the little side door.

A faint, metallic sound reached them, a key in a lock. Hatfield wasn't certain, but he thought that a stout figure, clad in black, was Barney Vale, come to put back the vital files.

Only two men went inside. The rest, perhaps four or five, lay down flat on the ground near the side door, to wait and guard.

Everything had been arranged with the proper authorities, by Captain McDowell. The back door was open, and Hatfield, Mc-Dowell, and the sentry went in. They tiptoed through the long corridors toward the file room, guns ready.

A faint light filtered from the high stacks in the file room. Somebody was in there, and they could hear the noises of papers rustling.

The intruder had a bull's-eye lantern. Hatfield, in the lead, crouched low as he went through the open entry from the hall, saw its stab of yellow beam.

"Hightail, boss!"

The shrieked warning came from the left. A man had been standing just inside the door, and Hatfield's ear rang with the shrill cry the man uttered.

Hatfield whirled. A pistol flamed almost in his face as he threw himself around in a desperate attempt to bring his Colt into play.

From behind him came the blasting roar of McDowell's Frontier Model. There was a howl of agony, and the second explosion came from the enemy gun that slanted down.

Hatfield let go a breath later, and hit the wounded killer before the man struck the floor.

The bull's-eye snapped out. Hatfield vaulted the counter separating the public section of the file room from the office where the clerks held sway. McDowell came after him, almost on Hatfield's heels, rolling over the barrier with cursing grunts.

A gun flamed from down the way. Hatfield replied, as McDowell jostled him, trying to beat him to the kill.

The two Rangers rushed their opponent, pistols snarling. The flying lead drove the man around, toward the corner. There were windows here, but they were barred.

"I'll go around the other way, Cap'n!" yelled Hatfield. "Don't let him past on this side!"

McDowell was gasping for wind. The exertion was too much for him. But he was chuckling in delight at being in the fight.

"Trust me, Ranger!" he panted, edging

forward.

A slug whirled dangerously close, burying itself in the wooden shelf close to McDowell's head. Hatfield ran swiftly around to the end of the high shelves. His quarry was dodging in and out, seeking to maneuver so he could get out the door, the only way out!

CHAPTER XV
GREAT DREAMS

One narrow shaft of moonlight coming in a window touched the Ranger, and bullets burned about him. He shot back at the flashes, and rushed through the aisle, driving his enemy before him with the fury of his Colt.

"Reach, cuss yuh!"

That was McDowell, calling on the cornered rat to surrender. It was a Ranger axiom always to give even the worst outlaw a chance to throw down his gun and surrender. At the same time, this offered the vicious a chance to take a first shot at the officer who showed mercy.

At the turn, Hatfield heard blasting guns, the curses of fighting men. He feared McDowell had been hit, as he heard a shrill Rebel yell pierce above the tumult. Teeth gritted, the tall Ranger swung to the end of the stacks. By the flames of the guns, he could see his captain and the burly, black-clad killer who, head down, was duelling with McDowell.

Hatfield fired, and McDowell jumped forth, his pistol blaring. The man went down, as McDowell landed on him with both feet. The guns ceased their stunning explosions, and then the Ranger had hold of the stout man's arms.

"He's dead, Cap'n!" announced Hatfield.

"*Bueno,*" growled McDowell. "He asked for it."

Shouts and gunshots came from outside. There were fighting men waiting for the file thieves, and so few of Vale's men that they would have their hands full and be unable to come in for an attempt at a rescue.

Hatfield struck a match. The little yellow flame came up. The black-clad figure crumpled on the floor lay on his face, and McDowell, biting his lip, was leaning against the wall, head down, blood streaming from his cheek.

"Cap'n — yuh're hit!" cried Hatfield.

"Ain't — nothin' but — a scratch." McDowell was breathing like a steam engine at work.

"You set down," ordered Hatfield. "Here's a stool. Easy, now."

"That — that was fine!" gasped McDowell.

When Hatfield made him sit down, McDowell closed his eyes, leaning back against the files.

The Ranger bent down. He rolled the dead man over on his back, and lighted another match. McDowell opened his eyes, to look. They stared at the fleshy face, the small eyes glazing in death.

"That ain't Barney Vale!" barked McDowell.

"It's Ince, Sam Ince, one of Vale's chief aides," growled Hatfield.

He felt sold, disappointed. He had expected to take the chief plotter himself that night, but the shrewd Vale had sent his helper, either because he feared there might be a trap waiting there or because he had had other important matters to see to. Ince was no doubt a trained land agent, instructed by Vale. Ince would have known where to replace the files.

"I was shore Vale would have to come hisself," said Hatfield. "I wonder where he is?"

Vale had fooled him, by sending Ince to Austin. Perhaps the land shark had come himself, yet —

He saw that McDowell was not badly injured. A splinter had cut his left cheek and from this the blood was flowing.

"Wait here, Cap'n," he said. "I'll be back

in a jiffy."

Outside, the recruits and sentries had swept up the handful of gun guards who had come along with Ince. They were plug-uglies, men who worked for Vale in Austin. They would answer no questions. Disarmed, surly, they were led off to the lockup.

There was real alarm in Hatfield's heart. Vale commanded plenty of guns. And somewhere in the vast territory to the west this man rode free, lashing with mad fury as he sought to smash through the meshes of the net the Texas Ranger had cast about him.

Keith Warden sang a gay range tune, something about his girl being a lulu, every inch of her. He puffed on a homemade cigarette as he leaned back in the sheriff's swivel chair, his booted feet up on the desk before him.

He was on guard at the little jail where Big Ed Pallette was dozing in his cell on the hard bunk.

Vanceville was just beginning to stir after the heat of the day — siesta time. The glaring yellow sun which sapped the energy of man when he was exposed to its direct rays, had slanted toward the Pecos and the great mountains in that direction.

Sheriff Al Craig was over at the Golden Horns. Jake Jervis, his Lazy J men, and some friends of theirs were at the saloons or yawning somewhere in the shade.

The world looked bright to Warden. He dreamed of Sue Garrett, of her beauty and sweetness. Soon he hoped to be with her again, when the Ranger had disposed finally of Barney Vale. Keith had a young man's confidence in the future, no doubt of his ultimate success in ranching.

"We'll pioneer," he mused, floating entirely free of his feet as he constructed his castles in the air. "We'll cross the Pecos and set up on a homestead range. I'll buy good breeders and improve the stock. Why, in a few years I'll be known throughout the West for my cows! Warden beef! That'll be me. Thousands of cows, at even just ten dollahs a head — why, it's a fortune.

"I'll even dress Sue in silk dresses and diamond necklaces. I'll wear me a forty-gallon hat, hundred-dollah boots, whipcord pants and a salmon-colored shirt. Folks'll point out at me and say, 'There he goes! That's Warden, King of the Cattle Empire.' "

In the slowly revolving grayish vapor from his cigarette, the events of his future life could be seen as plainly as though actually happening. A smile touched the cowboy's lips as he gloated over his success.

"When I got things rollin', I'll take Sue and the kids to Paris and London, mebbe even Rome! It'll be a picnic!"

In the excitement of sailing the ocean blue, he jingled the change in his pocket. It amounted to two or three dollars, for he had not been working for wages, and had, in his generous way, bought presents for Sue while in Austin.

"I'll send the kids to college, make 'em famous engineers. Their kids'll be born with golden saddles under their little —"

The bubble of his fancy was rudely pricked as Sheriff Craig came hastily into the office, followed by Jake Jervis and several other men.

The swivel chair hit the floor with a bang, jolting Warden back to reality. He had made the tour of the European capitals in record time.

"I got orders from Ranger Hatfield," puffed Craig, the heat and his haste having shortened his breath. He tossed a letter on the desk where Warden could read:

Sheriff Al Craig, Vanceville.

Come at once with every man you can muster. Vale and his main gang hiding at Shafer's Crossing in the abandoned house there. Will meet you on the road a mile north and lead you in the fight.

J. Hatfield, Lt., Tex. Rangers.

Warden's heart leaped. This was it!

"Let's see her again, Sheriff," requested Jervis. "Yuh positive it's Hatfield's writin'?"

"Looks like the other I got, the one I lost," answered Craig.

"Well, here's the letter the Ranger sent me," said Jervis.

He drew forth a folded sheet, straightened it out, and laid it by the note which had just been brought to Craig by a young lad who said a tall man had stopped him near Shafer's Crossing and told him to deliver the message in Vanceville.

They studied the two messages. Even Jervis was convinced.

"Yeah, it's the same hand." He nodded.

Already possemen were saddling up and checking their guns. Jervis had several Lazy J boys, and they would provide valuable assistance in the coming battle at Shafer's Crossing which was about twenty miles southeast of Vanceville.

"I'll saddle up!" cried Warden, starting out.

"Wait a jiffy," snapped Craig.

Warden turned in the door.

"Every cussed hombre in town can't go

along," said Craig. "Pallette's got to be guarded right. We may be out a couple days or even longer, if Vale moves. Hatfield'll be watchin' 'em and can lead us on their trail."

"That's right," said Jake Jervis.

"You stick here and take charge, Warden," ordered Craig.

"Aw, shucks, sheriff, let me go along!" begged Warden.

"No. Yuh got a stiff shoulder and a rough run won't help it any. Jervis, you stay, too, and help the kid. We need an older head here in case anything happens."

Jervis had been quite willing for Warden to stay but when told to do so himself, he was upset. But he had to accept Craig's dictum. It happened that Jervis, just before the note had arrived, had complained that he felt sick, and Craig had heard him. The sheriff wanted no lame ducks on the hard, fast trip to meet the Ranger and battle against Vale's bunch of outlaws.

Four older townsmen were deputized to assist in guarding the jail.

It did not take long for Craig to mobilize his large force of riders, and it was hardly four o'clock when they rode out of Vanceville.

Women and children were about, but the town seemed lonesome with so many younger fellows gone. Warden and Jervis stared after the risen dust left by the posse under Al Craig.

"That old sidewinder of a sheriff's jealous of me, I reckon," growled Jervis. "Afraid I'd show him up if I was along."

The town was quiet. Six o'clock came, and Jervis waited at the jail while Warden went over to eat at the lunchroom. Then the rancher took his turn. The other detailed jail guards were close at hand, where they could be quickly called. When dark fell, they would sleep at the lockup.

It was still light but the sun was sinking low in the sky. Warden smoked one cigarette after another, rolling them with expert fingers. Jervis was sitting on the sill, his legs sticking from the office door.

"Huh!" grunted the rancher suddenly. "Looks like they're comin' back already, Keith."

"What yuh mean?"

Warden left his chair and went to stand at the door, looking over Jervis.

Dust showed in the south as a large party of riders galloped into Vanceville. Warden waited. He could see only the rising clouds thrown up under beating hoofs, as the buildings cut off his vision.

Suddenly Warden uttered a sharp cry of

warning.

"Holy smoke! Come inside, Jervis! It's Vale's bunch!"

The rancher was galvanized to action. Warden was whistling shrilly to call the deputies. Jervis sprang to the door connecting the office with the city hall, and bolted it. He checked the barred windows, and hid the key to the cell-block under the sheriff's desk.

He had his six-shooter, and there was plenty of ammunition. On a rack on the wall were sawed-off shotguns, a rifle, with cartridges and shells in a wooden box. Jervis snatched the carbine, threw in a shell, and stepped to the still open front door.

The four deputies were trotting across the plaza toward the jail, in answer to Warden's whistling.

"I see Barney Vale!" cried Jervis.

Warden recognized others, too, toughs he had encountered in the fight against the land shark.

Vale was back among his outlaws — thirty to forty heavily armed killers, well-mounted!

CHAPTER XVI
SIEGE

Flaming guns began blasting. A deputy stumbled, and fell. One of his friends who stopped to help him up was slashed by a dozen slugs which threw him over the first man, dead. The other two made the front door, as Jervis and Warden opened fire on the van of the attackers.

"Lock that door, cuss it!" snapped Jervis, jumping back.

Heavy bullets whipped into the wood, shrieked through the opening to lodge behind them. Warden slammed the heavy oak portal, and threw the inch-wide bar bolt into place.

The windows were barred and narrow, the walls of three-foot thick adobe brick.

"They've come for Pallette!" declared Warden.

"I don't doubt it," Jervis said grimly. "We got to hold 'em. We better each take a wall. If they try to bust through from the city hall, we'll have to barricade and do our best."

Warden peered from the corner of a front window. Rapidly Vale's horsemen had looped out, taking over Vanceville with their guns. They swept past the jail, firing in, whooping it up like Indians.

Jervis swore in quiet satisfaction. He had made a hit. Warden's carbine crackled, and the killers outside, moving fast, checked the fact that the jail was closed up, and armed men were inside.

There was a lull as the building was surrounded. The four inside the office could hear men moving in the city hall annex, and the door was softly tried.

"I'd like to pick off that Vale tarantula," growled Warden.

But Barney Vale kept well back out of danger from chance slugs.

Craig had emptied the settlement of its best fighting men. Vale overawed or outshot what few tried to fight. In the jail, the men there heard a few gunshots from other parts of town, but soon all quieted down.

Dark was at hand. Jervis, crouched by his window, said:

"They're waitin' for night, boys. Then they'll rush us."

The four men trapped in the office waited for the shock of an all-out attack. They had good cover, but heavy posts, used as battering-rams, could breach any wall.

The day ended, plunging Vanceville into darkness. The moon was not yet up.

Listening with straining ears, they again heard noises from behind the door which led into the city hall. Then a cold, harsh voice called:

"You in there! I want to talk with Keith Warden."

"I'm here, Vale," growled Warden.

"I saw you. That's Jake Jervis with you, isn't it? Howdy, Jervis. You did a nice job fooling me, in Austin. I suppose the Ranger made you try it."

"Yuh're a clever cuss, Vale," rumbled Jervis, "but Hatfield'll dehide yuh and sell yore fat for tallow."

"We'll see," said Vale. "As to you boys, I don't care. I want Pallette, though. Turn him over and I'll ride and leave you free. Otherwise we'll have to smash in and take you all."

"Try and do it, Vale!" boasted Warden.

"It won't be too hard," said Vale. "Not with explosives."

A coldness touched Keith Warden's heart. He had not thought of that. If they had blasting powder and caps, or could find such in town it would mean death for them all.

"We'll fight to the end, Vale," declared Jake Jervis.

"You've asked for it and you'll get it," Vale said coldly.

A few minutes later, they heard the heavy thudding against the cell-block outer wall.

"Who's that — what's goin' on?" Pallette sang out to them.

Warden went through with the key, into the block. Pallette, his leg in a splint, was tossing on his cot.

"It's Vale, come after you, Ed," Keith said.

Pallette swore.

"He'll kill me soon as he's through into here! Give me a gun and let me fight it out!"

"That ain't a bad idea," said Warden.

Keith Warden called Jervis, who nodded.

"Let's carry him into the office," suggested the rancher. "He can lie on the floor behind the desk and watch that connectin' door."

They lifted the groaning Pallette and took him into the office, laid him on a blanket, and gave him a six-shooter. Then they locked the cell-block gate again, and Jervis and Warden took stands at either side of it. The wall would protect them, and they could fire around the edge through the heavy bars when the enemy entered the cell-block.

It was black inside. The ominous *thud-thud* of the thick post being used as a battering-ram shook the building, and each time it hit, it startled the men in there anew.

Neither Warden nor Jervis felt like bragging. Though they knew they could kill several of Vale's gunhands before they would be overcome — provided no explosives were used to stun the defenders. They could only hope and pray that Vale had nothing in that line with him, and had not found any in town.

"How yuh reckon Vale savvied to strike, just at this time, Jake?" Warden asked, in a subdued voice.

"Huh?" said Jervis. "Why, I believe that note was a drawoff."

"But the writin' — yuh said yoreself it was Hatfield's!"

"Looked like it." Jervis shook his head. "But yuh savvy Vale is a first-class forger, don't yuh? Such a scalawag could imitate any hand."

"That's right! But where would Vale get a sample of Hatfield's writin'? He'd have to —" Warden broke off with a curse. "The note the sheriff lost! Vale had spies here in town. They picked up the Ranger's message where Craig dropped it!"

"Yuh got it," agreed Jake Jervis. "Shore."

Warden sought for crumbs of comfort in the situation. He knew that Vale would kill him, and kill Jervis and Pallette. Of course, Hatfield would still be on the land shark's trail — unless Vale managed to dry-gulch the Ranger.

"If he catches Hatfield, and mebbe Craig, there won't be anybody able to fight the lobo," the young waddy thought. "Then he kin deal with Tate, and the Garretts, and anybody he wants to, any way he wants to."

"Heaven help Texas, if that sidewinder Vale wins out!" said Jervis suddenly.

The rancher had expressed Warden's sentiments exactly. He wanted to live, to be with Sue. Life which had looked sweet, looked even sweeter as the chance of survival dimmed in the cowboy's heart.

"They're through the wall," said Jervis after a while, his jaw tight and hard.

Falling stone, the lighter noises made as splintered bricks were easily knocked aside, came to them. They saw the widening breach, the faint outline of the hole.

"I'm goin' to sting 'em!" whispered Jervis.

He raised his shotgun and sent two blasts of buck from his shotgun at the opening. Men screamed. The flying shot had slashed as it spread, driving them from the hole.

Then came the reply — six-gun bullets, and answering buck which spattered all about the grille. The two men who guarded it had to keep back, for the air was full of death zipping through the bars or spattering as it struck the metal.

Under this fire, bolder gunslingers entered the cell-block. Quickly they discovered that the prisoner was gone.

There was a parley, then the heavy *thud-thud* of the battering-ram began at the connecting door into the office. The desk was shoved against the portal, but soon the wood began to splinter.

Warden and Jervis, the two deputies, and the crippled Big Ed Pallette gripped their guns, waiting to take as many along as possible when they died in the death rush. . . .

On Jake Jervis's splendid black gelding, Star, the Texas Ranger made good time in his return to Vanceville, as he frantically sought for some sign as to Barney Vale's movements.

Hatfield had been unable to get even a hint of where Vale had run to, or what his next plans might be, from the handful of sulky toughs he and McDowell had captured at the General Land Office in Austin. Either the outlaws did not know — as they kept repeating — or they were unwilling to jeopardize their chief's chances of eluding the law. For with Vale loose, there was always a hope they might be rescued one way or another.

Only by figuring out what his enemy would be likely to do, had Hatfield made his decision to run for Vanceville and the heart of the district in which Vale had been operating his evil scheme.

There was that second idea he had had — that Vale would seek to dispose of Big Ed Pallette. The rancher was the most dangerous witness against Vale, with the exception of the Ranger. Either of them could convict the land agent.

Star was not so well-trained to Hatfield's hand and mind as was Goldy. He could not be. Star was a clever horse, however, a fine runner with plenty of stamina. He had stood the trip well.

Several miles back, Hatfield had taken the southeast turn off the eastwest trail. A sign there said: "Vanceville — 15 miles." The road was poor, full of holes and protruding rocks. There were few good highways in the central and western section of the state.

"We shore need some better roads," thought the Ranger, as Star nearly went down in the dark shadows covering a deep ditch across the way.

He had an uneasy feeling that Vale was ready to strike, that danger loomed. It urged him on, to more and more speed.

The moon was up, but this accentuated the black spots. He slowed a bit, straining ears and eyes ahead. Goldy always gave him warning when the sorrel scented trouble, strangers near, but Star had not been trained for that however.

Star seemed eager, he kept pulling at the bit.

Hatfield reared the black as a man jumped out on the road, and the moon light glinted on a rifle barrel.

"Halt!"

Hatfield jerked on the left rein, as the challenger let go with a hasty shot which missed entirely.

"Hey, Sheriff — Lazy J — thisaway!" shouted the fellow in the road.

"Hold it!" called Hatfield hastily. "Is that Craig and his party?"

"Yeah, yeah! Who are you? Why didn't yuh halt if yuh're a friend?"

"I ain't in the mood to give in easy," drawled the Ranger. "Send Craig out. I'll talk to him."

Soon Craig's voice, thick with sleep, hailed him.

"It's the Ranger, Craig," Hatfield replied. "What yuh doin' out here this time of night?"

"What are we doin'!" Craig was amazed. "Why, we run to Shafer's Crossin' at yore command!"

Hatfield pushed back on the road. In the faint light he stared down at the thin face of the old sheriff.

"My command?" he repeated. "I just come from Austin. I sent yuh no orders."

Members of Craig's posse, camped in the bush, were coming out now, collecting around the Ranger.

"We waited around Shafer's for hours," insisted Craig. "We scouted and found the house at the Crossin' was empty, no signs of anybody havin' been there. I left two men hid nearby with a message for you, and we started home. When dark fell we was tired, and our hosses wore out, so we figgered we'd camp the rest of the night and go back in the mornin' — if you didn't show up."

It all came out. Hatfield heard the whole story. And learned that Warden and Jervis had been left in Vanceville!

Hatfield's anxiety mounted with each word.

"That note was a drawoff, Craig!" he said abruptly. "Vale may be in Vanceville right now! Rout out yore boys and foller me!"

"But the handwritin'!" wailed Craig.

"Vale's a clever forger. That's his business. Hustle! I'll go on ahead."

Hatfield spurted past the deputies, along the pitted, rocky trail, flogging for Vanceville.

Star, the black gelding, had made a fast race from Austin. He had strength, but not Goldy's staying powers. By the time Hatfield sighted the lights of Vanceville, foam stood out on the usually sleek flanks, and Star's breathing came hard. Still he drove on, loyal to his blood, his training. He had a brave heart.

On Hatfield's breast glinted the silver star on silver circle, emblem of the Rangers. His carbine and six-shooters were loaded and ready as he flashed straight into Vanceville.

The wind of speed whipped at his Stetson brim, and the hat tugged at the chin-strap under his rugged jaw. His gray-green eyes had the cold quality of the icy depths of an Arctic sea. Sitting easy in the saddle, he stared ahead, and he could hear the gunfire.

It came from the jail!

There were dismounted men about the city hall and calaboose. As he approached, spurting along the main highway, he was fired upon from the sidewalk, but he was moving fast and the bullets only sang near him.

He veered, turning Star onto the plaza, and bore down on the lock-up.

In the rear, where the cell-block was, he saw the gaping, black hole that had been smashed in the wall.

"Wonder if they got Pallette!" he thought anxiously, sizing up the situation as he moved.

Figures in Stetsons and sombreros, leather clothing and spurred boots turned to fire on the Ranger as the shrill alarm went up.

Alone, Hatfield charged straight at the enemy.

"Barney! Barney! It's the Texas Ranger!"

A stentorian-voiced lieutenant howled the warning, above the noise of the rising guns.

There was not the slightest doubt it was Vale, and his gang. As Hatfield had surmised, they had drawn off Craig and the possemen, then attacked. A gun spurted flame from a barred window. Hatfield knew that spot was the sheriff's office.

"Some of 'em are still alive and kickin'!" he thought, hope rising. "Now we'll see!"

CHAPTER XVII
ENCOUNTER

Daring outlaws held Vanceville. The citizens were in their homes, not daring to take a step outside for fear of a death bullet.

Several patrolling killers, who had been riding up and down the streets, converged toward the plaza at sound of the new alarm. There were hired guns behind every spot of cover surrounding the jail, and evidently more inside the city hall. Lanterns moved in the windows, but somebody in there let go with a blasting shotgun or barking Colt.

Guns were swinging on the Ranger. He heard lead in the air, and his Colts blazed back. The dismounted sentries around the building, while they had protection from the fire of the men inside, were exposed to Hatfield and he stung them hard. Some jumped up and ran away, toward the oak clump nearby.

In a window, as Hatfield tore past at the black's top speed, he thought he glimpsed

Barney Vale's stout figure, as the boss was framed by the lanternlight. Vale, at the insistent alarm, had run to the opening, close to the wall between the lockup office and the city hall.

Hatfield tried for Vale. Vale ducked back, out of sight. The mounted patrols were coming at the officer then, and their guns snarled.

The Ranger could only hope to delay them long enough for Craig to bring his large force into action. He could not hope to overcome so large a force of killers single-handed. He rode on across the plaza, swerved as he saw two horsemen coming his way. He knocked one man from his saddle, and the other slowed, to swing away.

Star slid in the dusty street as he made a pivot, obedient to Hatfield's tug at the reins. The Ranger cut out to the plaza, along the other side, with the front of the calaboose and city hall to his left.

Curses and gunshots hailed his reappearance. To his right, he saw the big collection of saddled mustangs, which must have brought Vale's bunch to the settlement for the night attack. The horses were being held by dismounted outlaws. There were thirty to forty horses and without hesitation he charged. Like a mad centaur he tore at the mounts, whispering as he came. His Colts blared, and a stinging slug sent a man holding a bunch of mustangs staggering and screaming.

The mustangs were already excited by the din, and now the shrill Rebel yell of the Ranger, his deliberately created hubbub, started them snorting, dancing. A couple of men with the animals dropped bunches of reins, to whip up their guns and try for the shadowy rider. Then the mustangs broke, running every which way in a blind stampede.

Barney Vale ran out the open double doors of the city hall, shouting orders to his men. It was a calamity to such fellows to see those horses, on whom they depended to make their escape, disappear. Yelling, outlaws ran for the mustangs, trying to snatch at the flying reins of the running animals.

Mounted patrols from the town were coming at Hatfield over the plaza now, and they pressed him away from the adobe walls. He saw a gun flash from a barred window in the front of Craig's office.

The sweated black gelding heaved under him, casting lather specks from his wet flanks. The Ranger slowed, moving around a line of buildings along the street south of the plaza, to give Star a breathing spell.

Three mounted killers who had been keeping the citizens under their guns tore around the corner after the tall officer, and there was a brief exchange of shots as they drove him onto Main Street.

Perhaps Vale thought by now that the Ranger must have help close behind him to make him so daring. At any rate, as Hatfield cleared the other end of the houses, he glimpsed Barney Vale running full-tilt across the wide, dusty road. Vale ducked under the continuous hitchrail, fully aware of the bullets kicking up the dirt, flicking the wooden posts, as Hatfield took long distance cracks at him.

Then Vale rushed into the Golden Horns, out of sight of the Ranger, who was pushed away from the plaza by patrols who were converging on him. Vale had had about a dozen of his men riding the streets to keep down any organized resistance. Those patrols had made it plain that any man who stuck his head out was liable to have it shot off.

A shrill cowboy whoop trilled on the warm night air. It came from northeast of Vanceville, from the rough dirt trail over which Hatfield had arrived in town.

His heart leaped. That yell heralded the approach of Sheriff Craig and the fighting men under him, the young fellows of the town and the Lazy J outfit. Cutting off, to elude the patrols, Hatfield had a vista up the street. Riders were charging toward the city hall and calaboose, and the Ranger knew they were Craig's men.

Panic seized the gun-fighting outlaws. They ran from the city hall, deserting their posts around the building. Firing opened up the moment Craig's boys sighted the enemy. Groups of dismounted killers were swiftly run down, and either surrendered or ate lead. The sheriff, panting from the exertion, galloped up, roaring orders, his floppy mustache bristling, his Colt barking.

The patrols who had been after Hatfield quickly saw what was occurring. They quit the chase, and cut away southward, attempting to escape while there was time.

Intent on catching Barney Vale, Hatfield spurted toward the Golden Horns, straight along Main Street. He ran inside, leaving Star with reins dropped at the hitchrail. A pale-faced bartender peeked gingerly over the top of his counter, recognized the Ranger and the star.

"Outlaws, bandits — they're holdin' the town, Ranger!" he gasped.

"They're cooked now!" Hatfield yelled back at him. "Pronto — did yuh see Barney

Vale — the stout hombre who just come in here?"

The barkeeper pointed to the rear.

"He run on through, Ranger. I believe he headed for the stable."

Hatfield barged out through the swing-doors at the front, mounted Star, and cut through the side way to the back street. Not far off was the corral belonging to the livery stable where he had boarded Goldy in order to allow the sorrel's wounds to heal.

Somebody was yelling down there.

"Hey, that ain't yore hoss! Come back!"

Hatfield swung Star that way. A wrangler was dancing up and down, shaking his fist after the disappearing figure of a rider, rushing south out of Vanceville.

"Was that Barney Vale?" demanded the Ranger.

The wrangler stared at the tall man on the lathered black.

"Mebbe. He stole the best hoss we got here, a golden sorrel! Say, you're the Ranger! Stout feller I've seen around town snatched yore sorrel. There he goes!"

Hatfield was already moving on Vale's trail. He made the corner, glimpsed the man ahead, spurring and flogging Goldy with a vicious quirt. The mettlesome sorrel was fighting the bit. He did not like strangers to ride him, but Vale was beating him into line unmercifully.

Fury clutched at Hatfield's pulsing heart. The black was almost done. His head dragged, his gait was slow. Star was trembling with exhaustion beneath the mighty Ranger. He could not even hope to hold his own with Goldy, even though the sorrel must be stiffened from injuries.

The Ranger rose in his stirrups. He dared not fire at Barney Vale, who hugged low over the gelding. Slugs sent in the dim light, at such jolting speed, might well kill Goldy instead of the thief.

Hatfield whistled, shrill blasts which reached Goldy's keen ears. The sorrel slowed. Vale beat him with the quirt and dug in the cruel rowels, but the gelding twisted in the air, reared back, fighting with all his fury. Vale had to use all his knee strength, and clutch at his saddelhorn to keep his seat. The next instant Goldy went down, rolling, seeking to pin the killer under his weight.

Somehow, Barney Vale got clear. He was up, limping, for his leg had been half-crushed as the heavy sorrel had pressed and twisted it.

A gun flamed, and Star faltered, turning from it as Hatfield left the leather and hit the ground running.

He could see Vale with hypersensitive clarity in the moonlight, the gleam of the clenched teeth, and the fire of the hard eyes. The stout figure crouched, Colt drawn, shooting it out with the advancing Ranger.

"Throw down, Vale!" shouted Hatfield. "You're under arrest!"

For forgery, perjury, for worse crimes against the people of Texas. Vale had killed, taken what he wanted.

"Ranger!"

It was a single word, but its screaming, high-pitched tone expressed Vale's burning hate for the man who had smashed his plans of empire, run him to this.

Vale fired again at the charging officer who had offered him a chance to surrender. The Ranger's heavy Colt blasted. Vale turned, writhing with the shock of the lead in a vital spot. He still gripped his gun, and it went off, but the flare was downward and the bullet entered the sandy earth.

Vale collapsed. Goldy had got up, shaken himself. The golden sorrel uttered a screech of rage, charged his enemy, drove his hoofs again and again into Vale's body.

"Enough, Goldy!" growled the Ranger. "The cuss is dead!"

Barney Vale was finished, done in, a heap

of flesh and clothes on the plain. . . .

Back at the city hall, Hatfield found the men who had fought with him in full control. Prisoners, toughs who had ridden for Barney Vale, had been herded into the cells, and guards had been placed on them.

A light shone in Craig's office. Hatfield entered. Craig hailed him, and there was Keith Warden, shaken, stained with blood running from many cuts, and yet not much hurt. Jake Jervis held his right arm limp, for it had been injured by a flying chunk of buck which had sliced it. A deputy lay on his back, his eyes closed. He had been badly hit.

The office was a shambles. Pallette was there on a blanket. He was grinning, however, and still living.

"It was some battle, Ranger!" exclaimed the rancher.

The door of the sheriff's office had been smashed in, as well as the door between the city hall and the office. But the defenders had made a barricade of the furniture. Bullet-holes decorated the walls and windows.

"Yuh come in the nick, Jim!" cried the excited Keith Warden.

Reporting to Captain Bill McDowell at

Ranger Headquarters in Austin, Jim Hatfield took a chair by the old officer's desk. McDowell was still feeling the effects of the scrap at the General Land Office. His system did not rebound as it had of yore.

"Yuh settled Vale's hash for him," growled McDowell.

"Yes, suh." Hatfield nodded. "Pallette'll get a jail term, Cap'n. He give me a hand and was willin' to help convict Vale. That stampeded that Vale sidewinder, and the judge should take it into consideration when he sentences Pallette. Big Ed is mighty sorry for what he done. He's asked Keith Warden to be his ranch manager while he's in the jug. Warden'll marry Sue Garrett, whose dad was killed by Barney Vale."

"Yuh savvy what Vale was after, don't yuh?" asked McDowell.

"Yes, suh. They're goin' to pass legislation runnin' a first-class highway from Austin to San Angelo, where there's nothin' but a bunch of dog trails now. It'll open up the whole country, and the lands touchin' the road'll jump way up in value. Vale wanted 'em. He thought he had a fool-proof scheme to get 'em, too, with the law on his side.

"He was familiar with the workin's of the Land Office and all, and snatched his big chance. He begun changin' the records and savvied just what to do. All he had to do was borrer a file, alter what he wished, and put her back. He did steal a key to a side door, but at first he didn't even need to sneak in nights, for they've been mighty careless up there, Cap'n. The system ought to be changed so's anybody who wants to can't stroll in and take out a file without close supervision."

"I'll speak to the governor at once." McDowell nodded.

"Wait a day or so," drawled the Ranger. "Vale done a lot of damage, and lawsuits and so on cost money. I got a list of pore folks whose places were took by Vale and his bunch. And before the system's changed, and those people have to go to law to prove their claims, I want to put things to rights, far as I'm able."

"I'll leave it to you," said the Ranger Captain.

"The Garretts'll get their home back. Frank can run the spread. Porter'll have his ranch, too, and so will others. I threw a real jolt into Larsen, who acted as Vale's dupe in Kimble County. That's why it took me a while to get back. I've been attendin' to all the messes left by Vale on the line from here to San Angelo."

When Hatfield had finished repairing the

damage done at the General Land Office, he again rode the golden sorrel on a warming morning toward McDowell's quarters. A newspaper on a stand caught his eyes with its black headlines.

He dismounted, bought a copy and stood scanning the story below the headlines which read:

State Legislature Passes
Austin-San Angelo Highway Bill!

"Well," he mused, "them folks who were put upon by Vale'll find theirselves mighty well off."

McDowell was waiting for him, restlessly pacing up and down the office. There was a dark look on the old Captain's face.

"Glad yuh're here, Hatfield!" he greeted abruptly. "Trouble — trouble! Always yuh shove one sidewinder out of the way, and there's another bobs up! Look at this!"

McDowell had reports from the southwest, across the Pecos.

"I'm ready, Cap'n," Hatfield said quietly.

He was glad to shake off the smells and dust of the city, mount the golden sorrel and head for the mighty wilderness, carrying the Law to Texas.

We hope you have enjoyed this Large Print book. Other Thorndike, Wheeler, and Chivers Press Large Print books are available at your library or directly from the publishers.

For information about current and upcoming titles, please call or write, without obligation, to:

Publisher
Thorndike Press
295 Kennedy Memorial Drive
Waterville, ME 04901
Tel. (800) 223-1244

or visit our Web site at:

www.gale.com/thorndike
www.gale.com/wheeler

OR

Chivers Large Print
published by BBC Audiobooks Ltd
St James House, The Square
Lower Bristol Road
Bath BA2 3SB
England
Tel. +44(0) 800 136919
email: bbcaudiobooks@bbc.co.uk
www.bbcaudiobooks.co.uk

All our Large Print titles are designed for easy reading, and all our books are made to last.